Prey for Dawn

A Novel

By
Christopher Michael Blake

To Bill,
thank you for
your support!
Beware the corner bar
Lucky at the
seven foot
fleet market!

Soft Cover – 10902
Published by Christopher Michael Blake LLC
Lanoka Harbor, NJ
www.Christophermichaelblake.com
2nd Edition
10 9 8 7 6 5 4 3

For my daughter,
who has taught me more about the responsibility it takes
to be a man than anyone else in my life.

Part One: Beginnings

1- Marc and Stacey

Marc Harden gazed at the time glowing on the dashboard in his car. The clock read 12:40 am. Marc let out a sigh and admired his wife sleeping in the passenger seat of the vehicle. He could hear her breathing silently, seeing her chest rise and fall, and returned his attention to the road before which was kicking up dust.

One really wouldn't call this a road. The road ended two miles back. What they were driving on now was more ground and muck embedded with pebbles of loose stone. The field of debris dust road ahead and lack of lighting impacted Marc's visibility. Dirt kicking up from the tires created a dust swarm surrounding his car, forcing Marc to slow down so he could maintain visibility. He noticed the last sign was five minutes back for a general store named Speedy's Restaurant and Grocery Store, which looked abandoned in the dark. Marc was hoping the road made up of gravel pebbles would lead back out to the highway, for if his wife, sleeping beside him, woke up, he would not hear the end of how they ended up lost. One wrong turn led to another wrong turn, then wrong turns.

The GPS in the vehicle having long since lost its signal, becoming frozen except for the circle searching for a signal. Marc watched the loop on the GPS go around looking for a signal. He was sure there was a name for this ring searching for the signal on the screen but couldn't think what the name was at this moment. The glitch with GPS had him miss turns, take unnecessary turns, recalculated wrong routes, and do too many U-turns to keep track of. Now the signal just roamed, moving in circles like a child on a merry-go-round
attempting to pick up a signal but never actually arriving anywhere.

Checking his phone using the light from the console, Marc also saw his phone had no Wi-Fi signal either. Marc was driving without breaks for twelve hours to visit family, his wife's mother in Tennessee. He started off driving from Texas through Oklahoma and now into Missouri. But now lost, Marc wasn't quite sure where they were or how they missed the highway. Now his bladder was on the verge of busting, and he needed to stop and urinate. The uncomfortable feeling on his bladder caused him to grip the steering wheel a little too tight. In the darkness, his knuckles turned a vibrant shade of red against the background of lights on the odometer. Peering through the windshield while the road ahead continued kicking up a barrage of dirt and dust. Hoping to see anything, he began to drive a little slower, looking for any type of signs or land markers, not wanting to turn around.

"Are we not there yet?" Stacy mumbled; her eyes still closed in the passenger seat beside him.

Marc glanced at her, hastily removing his eyes momentarily before responding, "No, I think we're lost."

To Marc's surprise, Stacey didn't even open her eyes when he said they were lost. She rested softly, eyes still closed, and he could still hear the sound of her breaths in a calm, monotone, gentle way. Marc removed his right hand from the steering wheel, placing his right on her left hand in a reassuring manner on top of her wedding ring and band.

"I hope you don't get too mad. But I don't know where we are." Marc said with bated breath.

Stacy opened her eyes, not fully realizing the gravity of what Marc said. She was about to say pull over at the next gas station and ask for directions, but when she saw the road throwing up stone and dust in front of them, she realized they were cast off onto an abandoned pathway. There were no gas stations, no diners, no interstate or highway, nowhere to stop and ask directions. In front of them and behind them was the darkness.

Cutting Stacey off before she became distraught at what was happening, Marc interjected.

"Please don't be mad. The GPS went haywire, and one wrong turn led to another, then another, and before I knew it, we were riding on this dirt road. I thought about turning around a couple of times, but we were making excellent time, and I just thought this eventually has to come out somewhere."

2

"It's ok. I'm not mad. How are we on gas?" Stacey said, more irritated than angry.

"We have plenty, at least three-quarters of a tank." Marc said.

"Then we'll be okay. Just drive a little further, and if we don't see anything resembling civilization, we'll turn around." Stacey began checking her cell phone as she spoke. There were no bars, no service, no signal, no signs of human life.

Marc squeezed her hand just a tad harder while trying to comfort himself as well. He took his eyes off the dirt road ahead, turning his head slightly to look into Stacey's eyes. In the glow of the dashboard light, Stacey returned his gaze but only for a second. In the darkness of the car, only half her face was visible, illuminated by the glow of the console, and at that moment, Stacey smiled, and Marc returned her smile. He knew he was in love with her even after all these years as he relaxed deeper in his seat. His bladder was temporarily forgotten about, and some of the tension melted away from his shoulders.

"There was a dinky food market back about five minutes ago, the market looked abandoned, but I saw a car parked in the back. Maybe I could turn around and bang on the..." Marc couldn't finish the sentence as something hit the hood of the car. Marc clenched the steering wheel with both hands, his knuckles bulging bright white as the windshield exploded with a bang and the glass spread cracking.

Slamming on the breaks following the impact on the hood. Marc's heart was pounding in his chest after having jumped into his throat. Afraid to move his shaking hands from the wheel, he gripped the steering wheel until his knuckles turned white for reassurance. Pushing the brake pedal down with his right foot with all his might. After the car skidded to a halt, Marc momentarily paused to breathe and think. If he removed his hands from the steering wheel, they would still have been shaking.

"Are you ok?" Marc asked, turning towards Stacey.
"Yes." Stacy said. They were both wearing their seatbelts.

"What was that?" Stacey asked. Streaks of blood on the windshield were visible on the shattered glass. There were no signs of what their car had struck or had caused an impact on their vehicle. Everything outside the car had fallen silent in the night.

"I'm not sure. Maybe some kind of animal. Things happened so fast; I didn't get a good look." Marc said.

Removing his seatbelt, Marc was about to get out of the car. "Don't go. Please. We can drive and go get help." Stacey said, placing her hand on Marc's as he held the buckle.

"What if I'm wrong and it was a person I hit. I'm pretty sure it was just a deer, but I should go check just to be safe." Marc said, trying to comfort Stacey as he removed his belt buckle.

"Marc, seriously, who would be walking around at almost one o'clock in the morning in the middle of nowhere?" Stacey said.

Marc reflected for a moment then grabbed his cell phone. There was still no signal as he tried to dial nine one one. He turned on the flashlight application, illuminating the front seat of the car with his cell phone.

"I'll be right back, sweetheart. Just keep trying to get a signal on your cell phone." Marc said, opening the car door and exiting the vehicle as he stepped on the desolate road.

Stacy watched Marc's cell phone light as she unbuckled her belt and turned in the car seat, keeping a visual on the light emitted from Marc's cell phone. Stacey kept trying her cell phone with no success. Not wanting to avert her eyes from the light of Marc's phone.

Stacy watched as Marc initially checked the rear of the car and then started walking back twenty to thirty yards in the distance. Eventually, Marc's silhouette faded in the dark. Her only visible landmark in the night was Marc's cell phone light. Stacey's eyes followed the light as it took a right turn into the tall fescue grass and then paused.

The light hovered motionless for one minute, then two; after three minutes of not moving, Stacey got out of the vehicle and stood at the open door of the car as she began calling into the night.

"Marc? Marc? This isn't funny." Stacey yelled, sounding more upset as her voice cracked through sobs while yelling. Hadn't she seen this in a horror movie? What was she supposed to do? The keys were still in the car, and the engine was still on.

"Marc, come back to the car." Stacey called out again, but there was no answer from a distance where Marc's light was.

She could see the stillness of the flashlight beam from the grass in the distance. Stacy thought back to all the horror movies she had watched and always chastised the characters for opening doors

4

and doing something stupid to get themselves killed. This thought gave her no solace but didn't negate that the keys were still in the ignition. She was sure as hell not going far from the car. If there was some psycho out there, she could lock herself in. On the other hand, what was she supposed to do, drive away and leave Marc?

But what if she was being overdramatic and he was hurt or caught in something. Maybe Marc twisted an ankle. She called for him again, with silence and darkness being the only response.

Stacey got back inside the car from the passenger side and climbed over the center console to the driver's seat. At least she was more competent than those girls in the horror movies, she thought to herself. Stacy placed the car in reverse until she was parallel to where Marc's flashlight beam illuminated the grass. The cell phone light was about twenty-five yards from the road.

She opened the car door and again yelled for Marc. "Marc? Marc, are you ok?" Stacey said as she hung out the open car door listening for a response.

Only silence and the floating dust from backing up the car hung in the air. Stacey placed her cell phone on flashlight mode and decided to carefully walk to where Marc's cell phone was shining. She did not want to rush in the dark and perhaps injure herself the same way as Marc had possibly done. At the same time, Stacey did not wish to linger any longer than needed. She thought about going as if she was removing a band-aid. It was best if she did it without thinking about it.

"Marc. God damn you. This better not be some practical joke." Stacey cried, holding back tears. Stacey left the car on, leaving the keys in the ignition as she started away from the vehicle, and at a rapid pace, she darted into the tall fescue grass about thigh-high. Through fifteen yards, nothing was visible in the dark. At three to four more footsteps, it was still too dark to see anything. Stacy's eyes were now adjusting to the darkness in front of her.

At three to five yards from where Marc's flashlight was, Stacey shined her flashlight on the spot on the ground where Marc's cell phone was emitting light, only Marc wasn't there. Stacey bent down to take a closer look at the cell phone and realized something was very wrong. Attached to the cell phone with the light illuminating into the sky was Marc's hand. Severed midway above the wrist, with no other signs of Marc except for the blood in the tall fescue grass. She gasped, taking two steps back, and while trying to

5

stop herself from throwing up and containing the fear, started to run back to the car. The realization of what Stacey saw didn't strike Stacey all at once. As fear gripped her, she began backing up before turning into a full sprint back towards the car.

Don't look back, she thought. Keep your eyes on the car. Just keep pushing forward, she thought. The car's headlights were fixed on the desolate road, and rays of dust played through the air. The interior light of the vehicle was on with the car door propped open. Just get to the car and go, Stacey thought. While she was thinking about the car and getting in and driving away, a humanoid figure leaped up from the grass on her right side, knocking Stacey to the ground. She had only glimpsed the figure lunging out at her in the dark; it was small, hairless, and albino.

Stacey landed on the ground with a thud. The wind knocked out of her, fright temporarily paralyzing her. She gathered herself, not sure where her pale assailant had gone away. She rolled over onto her stomach and realized she lost her cell phone during the attack. She could see the light coming from her phone through the fescue grass ahead of her. Beginning to pull herself up from the ground, she felt the figure grab her right leg as pain spiked into her calf. Stacey screamed, turning onto her back, and saw the albino figure near her feet biting into her leg. Without giving any thought as to what was attacking her in the dark. Stacey kicked the albino attacker in the middle of the face and watched it fall back.

Hurrying to her feet, Stacey tried to return to running to the car. Trying not to put any weight on her injured leg, Stacey found she could not push off her injured leg and run. Hobbling through the grass, a second humanoid smaller than the first jumped onto her back. Already off-balance, Stacey tumbled forward onto her knees and, trying to fight the smaller framed assailant, found she could get back up on her feet and keep moving towards the car. The pale humanoid was light enough for Stacey to carry on her back. But not being able to defend herself from the rear, her assailant began clawing with its long nails at her head and face before finally opening its mouth and biting down on the side of Stacey's neck.

Trying to fling her attacker off her back and defend herself, Stacey kept her eyes on the car down the incline in the distance. The car would be her place of safety. She could get help once she was in the car. Making it back to the car would end this nightmare. These were fleeting thoughts before another of the small humanoids wrapped her legs up from behind and bit down on her right hamstring. With the two attackers' weight and the injuries to both legs, she fell essentially helpless.

The blood loss was starting to settle in. Stacey's used her arms as she began to flail wildly at her dark monstrous assailants. Nothing human could or would do this to another person, she thought as she tried kicking and striking out at the albinos. They scavenged like a pack of ravenous dogs, picking off their prey, going for weakness, taking out the legs, Stacey thought. Another pale humanoid joined the feast and began to use its claw-like fingers to rip and slash across her stomach. She fought as the strength in her arms and loss of blood started to cause her eyes to shut permanently. Stacey's last thought was, how did this all happen so quickly?

2 - Jason Matthews

It was a silent Sunday, the first Sunday of fall. It was still too warm to have the leaves fall from the neighbor's tree and into your yard. Jason Matthews drove with the windows down. Next to him sat his wife Tammy in their Honda Pioneer Sports Utility Vehicle through North Dover, Georgia. Although fall had officially begun, the weather was not cold enough for a jacket but not warm enough to avoid wearing long sleeves. Jason, a history teacher at the University of Georgia, Tammy was a housewife who excelled at keeping fit and working out.

The couple could not be more different physically. Jason was tall, thin, ill-coordinated, and unathletic. Tammy, a blond with an athletic frame that accentuated the attractive features of her face. On this Sunday, the couple was enjoying their day off together at an outdoor auction. While Jason would enjoy looking over the historical items for sale, Tammy would just enjoy being in the open air and flirting with anyone who could catch her eye.

After parking the Honda Pioneer, the couple, holding hands, began the leisurely walk down the aisles of the historic memorabilia section of the market. Most of the memorabilia were knock-off-imitation, new or used junk, or flea market commodities. After an hour of walking to the end of the market was the auction section. A small auction stage with an auctioneer receiving bids from several near-empty rows of folding chairs. The chairs were previously assembled in rows but were no longer in order as people had moved them throughout the morning. Some people sat to watch the items being auctioned off as others sat to take a break from the morning walking. The smell from the nearby food trucks was deemphasized and over overpowered by the smell of urine.

While others waited in line for the pumpkin coffee or warm apple cider. Most chose not to pay attention to the man on stage rambling away trying to sell junk items at inflated prices. The auctioneer was an old man dressed in blue overalls with a long white beard. The overalls, like his hands, were dirty as auto mechanics would be.

"I'm going to get an apple cider. Do you want anything?" Tammy asked her husband.

"Maybe a bottle of water." Jason replied as he sat and watched the circus act of people bidding on what he considered frivolous items, items people would never use and just horde away.

As Jason sat and watched, several items came and went for bid, folding bicycles, furniture, clothing, boxes of DVDs, and cassettes. Nothing piquing his interest, most just discarded trash. Jason turned and looked toward the food carts where his wife was and saw her talking with another man. He noticed the palm of Tammy's hand briskly rubbing on the man's bicep. So maybe talking wasn't the correct word; serious flirting would more accurately describe the scenario. He turned and tried to pay attention to the auctioneer instead of leering or showing jealousy. Jealously or flirting were two parts of a conversation that, when brought up together, always ended in a fight between Jason and Tammy, so the topic was best to be left alone. Fighting and arguments tended to drag on in their relationship, exacting a high amount of emotional energy but leaving nothing changed and little resolved. Jason needed to make a conscious decision to avoid arguing, ignore the flirting and enjoy the day.

As Jason tried his best to avoid his wife groping the man at the cider stand, the next item at the auction came up for bid, and the auctioneer with the long white beard began his description of the product. Holding the microphone and moving around the stage, trying to gather enthusiasm for the following product, the auctioneer started the report. "Two mid-eighteenth-century chests. Locked and unopened for decades. Recently recovered from an attic and donated to charity for this auction. What could be inside, folks?" The auctioneer asked the crowd rhetorically.

"Confederate gold, silver jewelry, personal papers from Robert E. Lee, Civil War uniforms. No one knows but the buyer of these trunks and the starting price to find out is five hundred dollars. Do I hear five hundred dollars?"

9

The two trunks were shoddy. The paint had faded and peeled away many years ago. The leather straps long ago having been broken off. The brass hinges, lock, and ornaments were all speckled black and rusted over. Despite the age, the chests appeared unopened and sturdy.

One hand went up on the far side of the auctioneer stage. "I have five hundred." The auctioneer said. "Do I hear seven hundred and fifty?"

Another hand went up and another. "We have as thousand do we have fifteen hundred." Jason found himself making the next bid for fifteen hundred. What am I doing, he asked himself? Fifteen hundred, and there's probably just clothing and trash in these chests. Someone behind him bid higher, two thousand dollars.

"Two thousand dollars. I have two thousand dollars for these chests, and the contents can belong to the highest bidder."

Jason took this opportunity to raise his hand again. "Twenty-five hundred." Jason said, making the next bid. Jason's jealousy about his wife seething in the bidding. If Tammy could tease and get away with coming on to men, then Jason could focus his attention or inattention through spending money elsewhere. This was silly tit for tat; I'll get you back for flirting once you see what I bought and how much I spent.

"I have twenty-five hundred." The auctioneer continued. "Do I have three thousand?" He asked the small crowd.

Jason Matthews hoped to himself that he would not be outbid, and he would win the contest. He almost couldn't help himself. The surge and excitement of victory, even if minor. On the other hand, he had to ask himself what he was doing bidding on these trunks. Financially, this was far from a sound investment, and more than likely, he would be throwing good money out and end up with mostly a few pictures and worthless trinkets.

Then Jason imagined the conversation with his wife, Tammy. "Twenty-five hundred dollars!" He could already hear her nagging him. "Do you know what we could have done or where we could have gone for twenty-five hundred dollars?" Suddenly, wanting to avoid the possibility of the endless hours of nagging, fighting, and quarreling, Jason wished to himself please let someone outbid him.

The man with the straw hat and pointy white beard pounded the gavel and pointed towards Jason. "Sold! Please see the cashier with payment and to pick up your merchandise." The auctioneer said.

"What did you win?" The voice said behind him. Startled, Jason jumped out of his seat. His wife had just come up behind him. She had missed the entire auction but had arrived just in time to see he had bid and won something.

"Some trunks. Just some old trunks. Do you want to wait here while I pay for them?" Out of a daze and wanting to be semi-truthful, Jason replied while holding his breath.

It was as if Tammy were using some psychic ability that married couples have after years of knowing each other. Possibly, this could have been just plain curiosity, or maybe it was Tammy's propensity to see through Jason's bullshit. But when Tammy said, "No, I'll come with you and see what you bought." Jason felt deflated as if the wind was just taken out of the sails on the item he had just bid for and won. Instead of feeling ecstatic at offering the winning bid, he now felt ashamed at the purchase.

The auction had one cashier, an elderly lady with short white curly hair and glasses pushed to the far end of her nose. As he approached the elderly cashier, Jason thought she may have been the auctioneer's wife.

"That will be twenty-five hundred dollars." The cashier said. "No tax." She spoke. "The money all goes to a good cause for charity, so make sure you save your receipt for tax season." The cashier said with a smile through her ill-fitted dentures. Jason handed her his credit card. After being processed, the elderly lady returned the card and said, "You'll find your items to the right. Just hand the man your receipt."

She was a friendly lady, and Jason didn't want to turn around and look at his wife when she said the price of the trunks. Taking the receipt and signing the hard copy. He placed his copy of the receipt into the right pocket of his dark blue jeans.

"Jason, did I hear that woman correctly? Twenty-five hundred dollars? Are you insane? What did you buy?" His wife asked him, taking Jason by the arm and wrapping her arms around his as if she were not letting his arm get away. He could feel her clunky brown purse on his side, jabbing him like a thorn in his side.

They walked side by side, Tammy and Jason, to the long-wheel metallic cart, which was approximately six feet in length. On the cart sat the two locked, faded, and rusted trunks. With the

11

advanced aging of the locks, a minimal amount of effort would be required to break or smash into either chest. Jason handed the man with the name tag labeled Herb, who seemed to be overseeing the dispensing of the auctioned items, his receipt. Again, and not for the last time, Jason avoided looking at his wife, fearing the disappointment which would emanate from her fierce, fiery brown eyes.

Herb, the attendant, was an overweight man; taking the metallic cart the chests lay upon, he wheeled the six-foot-long cart down the dirt path back to the parking lot area and the Honda Pioneer. Herb was probably a former athlete in his high school days or his youth. Herb sported a huge bald spot and a very bad comb-over which the attendant kept adjusting back into its previous position every time the wind blew, picking up the leaves.

"The black Honda." Jason said, hitting the key fob button unlocking doors to the car. Herb, the attendant, wheeled the metallic cart to the back-hatch door, and Jason folded the rear seats down, creating room so the trunks could be stowed on the flat surface.

"You have to be careful if something breaks..." Herb said, letting the unfinished sentence hang in the air. As Herb squatted, picking up the trunks, Jason standing behind him, saw the ass crack of the overweight man. Plumber's crack was the official terminology, Jason thought. Has anyone ever looked at me like that, Jason thought, making sure his shirt, which was now covered in sweat, was neatly tucked in to avoid a similar fashion faux pas.

Jason got to the other side of the second trunk and successfully assisted the attendant in placing the chest into the hatchback.

"Thank You." Jason said as Tammy opened the passenger side door and got into the front. The attendant stood there for a second too long. Maybe he was expecting a tip? Jason wasn't sure if it was customary to tip an attendant helping carry items, he purchased at a charity auction. Jason shrugged off the uncomfortable pause, confident he would never see the attendant again, as he got behind the driver's wheel and started the ignition. As he backed out of the parking space, Jason could see Herb, the former high school athlete rolling the metallic cart back through the dirt path back to the auction.

3 – Jason Matthews

The drive home with Tammy was both frustrating and emotionally draining. Tammy started the conversation with the ever so pleasant "How could you spend twenty-five hundred dollars on two worthless pieces of junk?"

"It was an impulse buy." Jason said.

"Besides, we don't know they are worthless. There could be some precious items in there. The chests alone are probably worth one to two hundred dollars each. They are in good shape. If there are any historical documents or authentic civil war timepiece uniforms, this could be a scarce find. Who knows what kind of treasures we could happen upon when we open those trunks?" Jason continued.

"I just hope you are happy. You never think about anyone else. Everything you do is so very selfish." Tammy said, crossing her arms and glaring away from him out to the passenger side window.

The car grew silent, the way a vehicle can when two married people reach an impasse in an argument. The lack of conversation adding emphasis to the level of hurt and scorn felt by both parties. Further explanations or discussions would be useless. If a jury ever became involved, the winner would be announced when the trunks were opened, and the contents of the boxes sifted through. Until they got to the house, however, there would be restraint from both parties on engaging each other with words.

Jason pulled the car up to the driveway. Instead of lifting the trunks from the back of the vehicle and carrying them by hand into the house. Jason went into the garage and retrieved the dolly. Carefully placing the first trunk on the dolly and securing the first box with bungee cord cables, Jason wheeled the dolly into the house and up the stairs to his office, which sat on top of the garage. His wife went into the kitchen and took off her jacket while Jason went back out and retrieved the second trunk. He then undertook the task of taking each stair one at a time with the dolly behind him. While Tammy watched vacantly from the top of the flight of stairs next to his office.

"Are you alright?" Jason asked Tammy.

"No, I'm fine." Tammy replied as if awakened from a daze.

"You seemed like you were out of it for a second." Jason said as he wheeled the dolly with the second trunk past her and into the office.

"Just daydreaming." Tammy said.

"Honey, could you please get me a flat head screwdriver from the kitchen drawer and the eye-glass repair kit, so I can try and open these up without damaging the trunks." Jason asked as he removed his jacket and turned the desk light on. The October daylight was already fading, and Jason could see the sun withdrawing through the trees of the window on the second-floor study.

The study was an addition to the house, added on as a compromise to allow Jason to work and still be available at home for Tammy. Jason designed the interior of the study himself and prided himself on the view overlooking the entirety of the street and adjoining yards. The wood-burning fireplace was an addition that was very costly but supplemented the original feel of an actual study and office. The fireplace was an oddity, positioned over the top of a garage, but completed the sense of a true work-study. A place where Jason could get away and do work while being comfortable.

As his wife went downstairs to get the screwdriver and eyeglass repair kit, Jason knelt on one knee and examined the rusted locks on the trunks. Running his hands over the rough crevices of the tarnished brass lock and hinges, Jason thought how much effort would go into fully restored these trunks. He quickly blew into his hands; realizing he was chilly, he lit a fire in the fireplace and placed newspapers underneath the logs to help accelerate the burning and heat the room.

Tammy returned a few moments later with the flat head screwdriver and the eyeglass repair kit. She handed the tools to Jason, who thanked her and returned to kneeling and began the process of attempting to pick one of the locks on the first trunk. Tammy remained in the doorway, standing motionless, hawking her husband and awaiting the outcome of his expedition.

"What's the best-case scenario in terms of finding something in there?" She asked.

"I don't know. But purely speculating confederate gold would be nice. A long-lost letter from Robert E. Lee confirming his tendencies towards homosexuality would be priceless." Jason said jokingly with a smile. "But any kind of journals or uniforms would both be a historical winner and possibly given their condition financially rewarding." Jason continued struggling with the lock.

"Don't you think it's best we just rip the trunks open? I mean, you don't actually think you can pick that lock, do you?" Tammy said.

"What and ruin a perfect chest or treasure?" Jason said, and at that moment, as if on cue, the lock on the first chest popped open.

Tammy couldn't believe Jason opened the latch; Jason was far from handy or coordinated.

"How did you learn how to do that?" Tammy asked.

Jason, proud of himself and grandstanding, stood up and said a magician never reveals his secrets and pointing towards the lap-top open on his desk. The laptop was repeatedly playing on loop of a man picking locks with the sound off.

"You asshole." Tammy said with a smile, flirting, and in an instant, everything between them was okay. She had that effect on men, and Tammy's beauty during moments like this was one of the many reasons Jason married her, he thought.

"Let's see what we got in here." Jason said impulsively, lifting the lid of the first trunk without any thought. The damp mildew smell from the chest overtook him and made him momentarily turn his head away. Trying to breathe through the dank smell, Jason began taking the items out of the trunk, mainly containing clothing. Worker's clothing, two pairs of shoes, a few pictures, a harmonica, and a hat.

"Looks like we struck out on the first trunk." Jason said, disappointed, but we still have trunk number two to open. Tammy was beginning to lose patience as Jason started the process of picking the second lock. Jason took twice as long to pick as he felt the pressure of his wife's disapproving gaze. When Jason was about ready to quit and rip the lock off with the screwdriver, he heard the pop of the brass lock and, without show-boating, this time lifted the lid of the second box.

If the contents of the first trunk were disappointing, the contents of the second trunk were devastating. Ladies' undergarments, one boot, an umbrella, stockings, and a few dresses. None of which were worth more than a few dollars, let alone twenty-five hundred dollars.

"I cannot believe you paid twenty-five hundred dollars for this junk. You idiot." Tammy screamed.

"There has to be more here." Jason said, disbelieving searching through the items.

"You've looked through everything already. It's worthless crap." Tammy said before bending over and picking up the clothing and throwing the women's undergarments at her husband. "Face it. It's worthless. You spent twenty-five hundred dollars on utter rubbish."

"You act as though you contributed to that twenty-five hundred dollars. Like you worked for that money." Jason said, trying to contain his rage. The statement was a low blow aimed at the fact Tammy stayed home and didn't work, but the rebuttal and the harshness of the words had the desired effect.

Enraged, Tammy picked up the women's boot, stood up, and tossed the boot at Jason, striking him in the face. "I'm leaving for the night. Don't bother calling me." Tammy said, storming out and going down the stairs.

The effect of the shock of the boot to the face plus the rapid response of Tammy storming downstairs and out the front door froze Jason like a statue. He didn't mean to be hurtful or inconsiderate. He wished like hell he could tell his wife how he felt about her. But, by the time the initial shock of everything had worn off, Jason could hear Tammy's car starting in the driveway. Looking out the second-floor study window, Jason could see her car pulling away before the car disappearing into the distance.

Still standing, Jason began trembling. Going through various stages of grief all at once, disappointment, rage, anger, then going back through all the items from the trunk, laying them on the floor, before sorting over them again. Nothing. There was absolutely nothing of value here at all. Now his feelings turned to blame. "They knew this when they sold me the trunks. They'd been opened before." He began saying to himself.

Jason started to place the items back into the trunk to clean up his office area. He put another log onto the fire. As he finished putting the men's clothing back into the first trunk, he noticed something he missed going through the boxes the first time. Attached to the bottom of the lid of the first trunk was an envelope. The envelope was stuck in the wood crease of the trunk lid and had stained yellow with the passage of time. Visible on the front of the envelope was writing. Jason pulled the yellow faded envelope from the bottom lid of the trunk and began searching the lining of both boxes. Looking to see if there was anything else, papers, or other items he may have missed initially. There was nothing else. Only the envelope.

With his last bit of hope, Jason looked at the front of the envelope engraved with writing. The name *Jessie H. Hillman, Jr.* was written in ink upon the envelope. The name Jessie H. Hillman, Jr. wasn't a recognizable name or a famous name.
"Jessie H. Hillman, Jr.," Jason said out loud to himself.

With unsteady hands, Jason opened the envelope and pulled three pieces of folded yellowed paper out. He placed the envelope on the desk, sat down, and opened the folded pieces of paper. The first page was blank. The second page was blank. Lastly, the third page was blank. No writing, no scribbles, no drawings, nothing. All three yellowish pages were the same, empty.

Not having any writing on the letter was a crushing defeat. Finding a letter, Jason could have possibly salvaged something of value from the trunks. The blank pages seemed as if victory was snatched from his hands. Tammy was right, he thought to himself. Twenty-five hundred dollars was spent on two trunks, a bunch of costume jewelry, and three blank pages.

Defeated, Jason placed his head in his hands and tried not to cry. His wife had told him not to call. But maybe if he called and apologized, she would forgive him. He picked up his cell phone and found Tammy's contact number and pressed the dial button. The phone quickly went to voice mail. Tammy had turned her phone off. Should he leave a message?

"Hi, this is Tammy. You know what to do." The voice recording said.

"Tammy, it's Jason. I'm sorry, Hunny. I shouldn't have spent that money today, and I shouldn't have insulted you. Please call me back and let me know you're okay. I love you." Jason said into the phone before hanging up. Jason put his phone down on the desk, feeling ashamed about arguing but worse about the apology.

There was a flawed feeling in his heart or stomach about apologizing.

Sighing, Jason leaned back in his computer chair. The fire had been warming Jason's back and neck as the wind howled against the window of his office. Without realizing what he was doing, Jason held the three pieces of paper from the envelope in his left hand. Jason went to place the pages down on the desk and, after staring at the pages for more than a minute, reached for his cell phone and dialed a new telephone number. The phone was answered on the first ring.

"Hello." The voice on the other side of the phone said.

"Marcus, it's Jason. Look, I know it's getting late, but is there any chance you could stop by." Jason said excitedly.

"When do you want me to come by?" Marcus asked.
"As soon as possible." Jason said.

"I'll be right over." Marcus said after a brief pause.

4 – Abrams

It was a beautiful fall Texas day. The leaves hadn't yet started to change colors or fall from the trees, and it was still hot out. The last of the remains from summer. A day to enjoy and feel the sun beat down on your face and thank God you were alive.

That's what Abrams thought to himself as he stared out the window of the office he was in, watching the traffic drive by and the people walking at the park across the street. He thought to himself, it's a great day to be alive, as he opened the desk drawer and stared in. Not yet, Abrams said to himself the day was too early, not even eleven yet, still plenty of time for customers to come in. Abrams thought a customer wouldn't come in here, and he was trying to have willpower, so he prudently decided not to start just in case.

Abrams shut the drawer of his desk and stared at the clock on the corner of his computer monitor. Ten fifty-eight AM, the clock read. He sighed to himself and balled up a piece of computer paper and, with an air skyhook, threw the balled-up piece of paper towards the wastebasket he had positioned in the center of the room.

"Three points." He said out loud to himself as the paper ball missed the wastebasket completely and rolled under a desk on the other side of the room. At ten fifty-nine AM, there were already four different pieces of paper lying under the desk. Boredom. No, that wasn't right, Abrams thought to himself. Depression. Yes, depression. Now that was a more accurate word. A striking word. A word the average person could relate to and have empathy with. Depression.

Abrams went back to looking out the window at the sunny day and the joggers and bicyclists across the street. He sat staring through the window, looking at the people across the street living their lives, enjoying their day, and moving about. He was staring out the window when the car entered the strip mall where his office was and proceeded to pull into the parking spot in front of his office. A potential client, possibly.

The car was a blue two-door hatchback, not new and not clean. The car's owner was something else entirely, Abrams thought as he straightened the knot on his tie and gave his desk the once over. Searching for any incriminating evidence before this possible client walked in.

The owner of the blue two-door was a beautiful female with long legs, a mid-twenties brunette with long curled hair. As she exited her vehicle, she pulled her shirt down slightly, showing she was self-conscious about people looking at her body. She wore a pair of heels, a black pair of stockings, and a dark blue jacket with a black top underneath. A professional look. Someone with a day job struggling to make ends meet, Abrams thought to himself. Does she know how attractive she is, Abrams thought to himself, or was the attraction just her youth?

Abrams himself, in his mid-fifties, thought as he got older, more and more women became more attractive simply because of their age and youth. The older he got, the more attractive younger women around him became because they became more unattainable for an older man. There was that word creeping back upon him; Depression.

He shook the feeling off as the door to his office opened, making a beeping noise as the female client in her dark blue skirt and jacket entered the office area. There were four desks in the office, but only two were ever used and had computers sitting on them. Two chairs sat in front of each desk. Abrams desk was placed farthest from the door but next to the window looking out the parking lot. The lettering on the sign in the window with big letters read "Abrams and Butler, Private Detective Agency." The sunlight allowed the stenciled letters on the window to cast a shadow and fall through onto the floor as the makeshift trash bucket remained positioned in the center of the room. Because of the large office window, the office was bright during the day and allowed a large sun into the office area.

"Good morning." Abrams said, standing up and extending his hand.

The woman stopped suddenly, unsure. Insecure, Abrams thought the hesitation was about his height. Abrams stood only five feet six. The woman noticing the awkward pause, continued forward and shook Abrams' hand.

"Please be seated. Tell me, what brings you in today?" Abrams asked as he sat down.

"This is going to sound silly but are you a detective?" The woman asked.

"Yes, Ma'am, allow me to introduce myself. I'm Abrams." He replied with a slight chuckle.

"Fully licensed, insured, and credentialed. Before this, I was a police officer for the Texas Highway patrol for twenty years. So yes, Ma'am, I believe I can help you." Abrams said with a reassuring smile.

The woman removed her sunglasses, revealing deep blue eyes underscored with dark eyeliner, which made her eyes pop against her pale features.

"This is going to sound silly." The woman said.

"It always sounds silly at first, but I believe something is bothering you, and the consultation is always free, so please, the coffee may be bad but indulge me and start with your name." Abrams said, waving his hand, trying to add some levity and comfort to the conversation.

That makes sense, the woman thought, starting with my name. "Brooke. Brooke Mueller. Mr. Abrams, about a week ago, my sister, Stacey, and her husband took a trip to visit my ill mother in Tennessee and visit family. They left on Saturday, and today is Friday, and they haven't been heard from since." Brooke said.

"I am distraught; this is totally out of character for my sister or her husband to be away for this long, especially when people are expecting them and to be out of touch. It's almost as if they dropped off the face of the planet." Brooke said.

Abrams grabbed a pad and pencil, wrote down Brooke Mueller at the top, missing sister and brother-in-law below.

"What is your sister's name Mrs. Mueller?" Abrams asked. "Is it the same as yours? Mueller?"

"No. My sister took her husband's name, Harden." Brooke said, spelling out the last name.

"What is your sister's husband's name?" Abrams asked. "Marc." She replied, waiting for the next question.

"Were there any marriage difficulties between them, your sister Stacey and her husband, Marc?" Abrams asked.

"No. Not as I am aware." Brooke said.

"Has your brother-in-law's family heard from them recently?" He asked.

"Not that I know of, I spoke to his mother and father last night, and they are also starting to become concerned." She replied.

"Can you write down the names of any friends or family for your brother-in-law, telephone numbers, addresses, places of work, etc.? Things I can follow up on." Abrams said, handing Brooke a pen and paper.

"Do you believe her husband had something to do with them going missing?" Brooke asked unbelievingly.

"I can't rule it out. Ninety-nine times out of one hundred, when someone goes missing, the prime suspect is usually someone they know who caused them to disappear. An immediate family member becomes the number one suspect. Best to rule them out first." Abrams said.

"Have you filed a missing person's report?" Abrams asked.

"Yes. I filed a report here in Texas and another one via the telephone in Tennessee yesterday. But to be honest, they didn't seem much concerned about them. The fact I didn't know the routes they drove seemed to make the police much less interested." Brooke said.

"The police departments are overworked, and cases need to be assigned, and that takes time. The fact you don't know where they went missing could cause several different police departments to do twice the amount of work for people who may never have gone missing in the first place. If this was a kidnapping and we could prove it, this would be a different story. Going across the state lines would be a Federal offense. But right now, we don't know anything. What kind of car did they drive?" Abrams asked.

"A Grey Lexus, newer model. I have the license plate information written here along with the vehicle registration number." Brooke said.

"How did you get this information, the license plate and registration information from their vehicles?" Abrams asked.

"I went to their house here in the city and found a copy of the registration. I thought it would be useful when I contacted the police to provide them with as much information as possible." Brooke said.

"That's good. Very smart. Has anyone else been to the house so far?" Abrams asked.

"No, just me." She replied.

"I may ask you to meet me at your sister's house, so I can take a look through." Abrams said.

"I also have to be honest, Mrs. Mueller; private detectives are not cheap. If this was a cheating husband or a simple tail, we could limit the hours. But you..." Abrams paused for effect or emphasis, "If you decide to follow through and hire me to look into this whether they are found or not, all expenses, including gas, tolls, mileage, and our hourly rate, are billed weekly. This could get very expensive. I can promise I will give this case my full attention and not leave any stone unturned." Abrams said as he handed Brooke the hiring agreement letter.

"Mr. Abrams, I have a terrible feeling about my sister, Stacey, and her husband, Marc. I don't believe Marc had anything to do with her disappearance. For my sister's safety, I don't think this can wait." Brooke said signing the hiring agreement.

Before Brooke Mueller left, she signed the paperwork hiring Abrams to look for her sister. When she was gone, Abrams placed his feet up on the desk and tore a blank piece of paper off the notepad, crumbled the paper up, and threw the balled-up paper towards the wastebasket placed in the center of the room.

This time the paper went. "Hey, maybe this day was getting better." Abrams thought to himself. Of course, the day could always get just a little bit better. Abrams opened the desk drawer and pulled out the bottle of vodka and a paper cup, placing the paper cup on his desk. He unscrewed the top of the vodka and poured himself a shot. He put the lid back on the vodka bottle and placed the bottle back inside his desk.

Kind of predictable that an ex-cop should be a semi-professional drunk, he thought to himself as he stared at the contents of the vodka drink. Abrams picked up the paper cup and swallowed the shot in one gulp. Oh, that went down smooth, he thought. He wouldn't worry about another customer coming today, he thought, miracles don't happen twice in one day, he said to himself and chuckled, crushing the paper cup in his hand.

Abrams placed his feet back up on the desk and pivoted in the swivel chair to look at the map behind him. The large map hung on the wall behind him and was of the United States of America. All of the states, the terrain, sea level, cities, major highways, mountain ranges, and in-between. Not listed on the map were several thousand hotels, State and local police departments, vehicle repair shops, and a litany of other places to disappear in. Abrams thought, staring at the map.

Abrams had bought the large map, already framed at a yard sale for fifty cents. The map was placed on the blank white wall of the office to fill the empty office void. A certain gravitas he thought purchasing the map for only fifty cents, but substance, nonetheless.

Looking on the map, the task of finding a missing sister didn't look too daunting, but the area he was looking was large, certainly from Texas to Tennessee, only one state to drive through Arkansas with lots of states bordering them. Mississippi could be a possibility. Missouri also could too. Alabama was unlikely, but Abrams couldn't rule that state out. The thoughts of so many opportunities where people could go missing. So much land to cover and so many telephone calls to make, Abrams looked at the desk drawer one more time.

5 – Tammy Matthews

When Tammy stormed out of the house and sped out of the driveway, she smiled. She had been looking for a chance to get away from Jason. Those stupid trunks or chests had been the perfect cover. She couldn't believe Jason could be foolish enough to buy those for twenty-five hundred dollars. Time to put him out of mind. He would pay for that mistake as well, she thought as she stared in the rearview mirror at herself. She always loved looking at herself with her brown eyes, flawless face, and impeccable tight body.

Just now, the sun was going down. The light was growing dim, and headlights from passing cars began staring at her from across the other side of the highway. As she turned off onto the side streets, there were fewer and fewer cars. Pulling into the Bay View motel parking lot, the fluorescent light from the motel sign was faded, showing signs of depreciation. The motel may have been called Bay View, but there was no water around for miles, only the smell of the diesel trucks whose owners spent the night at Bay View on the cheap. The hotel was the kind of place women wanted to avoid going alone, and if a woman did go to the Bay View motel by herself, she was usually a working girl.

Tammy pulled her car up outside of rooms eleven and twelve. The last two rooms on the corner of the hotel. She placed the car in park and flipped the sun visor down, exposing the mirror. She checked her makeup one last time in the light and put the visor back down. She exited the vehicle and walked to room twelve. She could see the light coming from the television playing under the curtains as she knocked on the door.

Like a bolt of lightning, the door opened, and a man grabbed Tammy around her waist. Standing before her and holding her tightly by her waist, pressing his body tightly against her body, imposing his mouth upon her mouth in a deep sensual kiss. This is what Tammy wanted, Dominic Cross. Cross was dressed in a white ribbed tank top and cargo shorts, exposing his tattoos across his ripped arms. The same arms he held her in and refusing to release her with.

True to his name Dominic Cross had a tattoo of a Knight's Templar cross on his right bicep. Underneath the tattoo, the word SAVIOR was written. On his left bicep, the word written was Nomad and cloaked figure with a scythe riding on a motorcycle.

Cross picked Tammy up off the ground and carried her into room twelve while kicking the door closed with his left foot. Cross walked three steps with Tammy in his arms. Her legs straddled around his lower back as he threw Tammy on the bed. Neither of them opening their eyes, totally taken at the moment.

The kissing and the fumbling of clothes. Yes, Tammy thought.

He ripped her shirt off into two and began suckling on her breasts. Yes, she thought.

She began reaching for his belt and the button on his pants. Yes, she thought.

The passion of being locked together and being comforted in his strong embrace. Yes, she thought. This is what she wanted.

The repeated climax and withdrawal. She could breathe again. Yes, she thought.

When the passion had ended, the television still played in the background. A program about making steel weapons on the history channel with the sound off. They lay tangled in bed, half-covered in sheets and sweat as the air conditioner rattled in the background. She ran her fingers down his hairless chest and over his tattoos as he played with her hair. Cross always loved the way women smelled.

Being with Dominic wouldn't always be like this, she thought, this wasn't the first affair she had, and this would not be her last. But so far, this affair offered the most prolonged sense of titillation. She removed that thought from her head, best to stay in the moment.

"I have good news." Tammy said. "I can stay the night, and we can do whatever you want, for as long as you want, repeatedly." she said with a smile.

26

There was no mistaking the Neanderthal alpha male quality Dominic displayed in his smile and touch. Being with him offered a completely different sexual experience from her husband, Jason. She knew from the first time she had met Dominic Cross at all places the local gym. He was there working out, minding his own business, but in the mirror, he could not take his eyes off Tammy, and she had caught him looking at her several times. Cross was in no way subtle about looking at her. She supposed she had been checking him out too, and perhaps he had picked up on that. When the time to leave came, Cross purposely chose to walk out the door simultaneously as Tammy. As she was leaving the gym, Cross was standing next to her. He put his sunglasses on and turned to her, and said, "Would you like to get some coffee."

Ninety percent of the time, the answer would have been no straight off. But this felt different. Maybe Tammy was bored looking for a thrill, so she said yes.

"Follow me." Dominic Cross said, walking to his two-sixteen Harley Davidson Softail Breakout American, as he put his goggles and helmet on. She followed him in her car to the coffee shop down the street. During the conversation, Cross admitted without being embarrassed he was recently released from prison and was a ranking member of the Nomad motorcycle club. He also admitted that both experiences of being in prison and in a motorcycle gang were nothing like television, and both could be a little lonely.

His vulnerability and honesty touched her, and Tammy admitted that she was married but not in love with her husband. They talked about nothing for what seemed like hours, and in the end, they parted with a handshake.

"Can I have your number, so I can call you?" Dominic asked.

"No." Tammy said, playfully flirting with a smile.

"When can I see you again?" Cross asked.

"We'll have to be content that destiny will put us together again in the same place at the right time." The line was cheesy. She knew the line was cheesy. But Tammy felt the pursuit and chase were exciting parts of foreplay and could also be exhilarating, Tammy thought.

Destiny turned into the next day at the gym, Tammy came in at her usual time, and Dominic Cross was already there, lifting weights. As she passed by him on the way to the elliptical machines, she smiled, and Dominic said, "The day is way too nice to be indoors. Wanna go for a ride?"

"It depends? How long have you been here waiting for me to walk in?" Tammy asked as she stopped to talk with him.

"A little bit longer than I would have but not enough to be a stalker about it." Cross said shyly, smiling like a child caught doing something they weren't supposed to do.

"In that case, let's go. But you leave first. I'll follow you in five minutes. I can't take the chance anyone sees us together. I'm a married woman after all." she said.

Five minutes later, Dominic was already outside on the Harley Davidson with the engine roaring. He handed Tammy his motorcycle helmet, and once she sat on the motorcycle, she held him tightly around his waist as he put the bike into gear. He didn't go fast; he didn't need to. She held him tightly around the waist with no reservations because she wanted to. He took a nice leisurely ride through the country, through the farmland, enjoying the summer day. After an hour of riding, Dominic Cross pulled the motorcycle up a hilltop surrounded by corn and an orchard filled with apple trees. He parked the Harley Davidson in the shade and, with Tammy still on the backseat taking her helmet off, reversed positions to face her. Face to face. Body to body. Smile to smile.

She was almost ready to speak to break the silence when he kissed her. A long passionate kiss. He wasn't waiting to see if she objected. She didn't. They were both adults; there were no more games. After spending an afternoon of passion under the shade of the apple trees, he drove her back to the gym.

"We can't meet here at the gym anymore." She told him. Too many people know my husband and me.

"I'm staying at the Bay View motel in the next town over, room twelve. I pay by the month. I would very much like to see you again and hope this wasn't a one-time thing." Dominic Cross said.

The affair wasn't a one-month thing and instead had grown into a summer fling going into the fall. Now laying here at the Bay View motel with Dominic staying the night, she had the confidence to say how she felt.

"I want you to kill my husband." She said.

6 - Marcus Robertson

Marcus Robertson had difficulty driving at night without his glasses, and on this night, he had flown out of his house after hearing the sense of urgency on the other end of the telephone when Jason called. As the duck turned to darkness, the driving became more difficult due to his poor night vision. The drive took Marcus almost thirty minutes to the hill-top community where Jason lived from Marcus Robertson's modest apartment. About halfway there, Marcus wished he had taken his glasses with him before leaving in a hurry. Marcus found the glasses in his shirt pocket underneath the vest he was wearing as he neared Jason's house.

Upon pressing Jason on the phone to answer why this could not wait until morning, Jason was very coy and would respond with, "I need your help." Or "There was much to think about and contemplate, but I need you to be here ASAP."

When Marcus started his job at the university, he first met Jason Matthews. Jason was a professor of history. Specifically, American history. On his first day, Marcus arrived at the social studies department next to his department Anthropology. Anthropology is the study of humans, human behaviors, societies in the past and present with two main branches; cultural anthropology and biological anthropology. Marcus' main field was the latter, focusing on the study of the biological development of humans.

Marcus had been shunned by all the tenured professors during his first department meeting when Jason Matthews befriended him. The two quickly fell in step, having lunch with each other and Marcus taking Jason's advice on how to handle the faculty members at the University of Georgia. The two were rarely seen apart and developed a deep friendship. The other faculty members, being jealous or spiteful, took offense to their company together. Comments and name-calling the pair "Gilligan and the Skipper" referring to the awkward height difference between the much taller and thinner Jason Matthews and the shorter and plumper Marcus Robertson.

Because of this friendship with Jason, when Jason called Marcus and asked Marcus to rush over, Marcus did so with minimal hesitation.

Pulling his car into the driveway of the Matthews residence, Marcus was getting ready to shut off the headlights to his vehicle off. When Jason Matthews opened the door to his house, running down the steps in the dark and across to the driver's side door. Jason was in a much-hurried state, worked up in a frenzy. Marcus had known Jason through the years, and he had never seen his friend in such a rushed state before.

When Marcus exited the car. Jason gave him an uncharacteristic hug and whispered in his ear through the fall wind, "What I am about to show will change everything." This was beyond the usual greeting and was a bit off character with how Jason usually presented himself. Jason took Marcus by the upper arm with those words, guiding him to the house and up the porch stairs.

"What's this all about, Jason?" Again, Marcus asked him as Marcus became fearful when none of the house lights had been turned on, and Jason was asking him to follow him inside the dark house.

All of a sudden, Marcus feared the worst. Had he hurt or killed Tammy? He thought. The idea Jason may have hurt or injured Tammy was a fleeting notion but present in his mind, nonetheless. Marcus knew Jason and Tammy were having marriage problems. Jason had talked numerous times about his marriage problems. Holding his breath, Marcus followed Jason to the staircase leading up over the garage to Jason's office. Marcus could see the light emanating at the top of the stairs from the open door of the study.

Following Jason, he came up to the study and observed the two open chests on the floor with a mess of clothing heaped into them. The desk was chaotic, and a fire was roaring in the fireplace. A little bit lost for words, Marcus couldn't think of anything to say, and Jason turned to him and asked him to have a seat at his desk in one of the parlor chairs.

"What is this all about?" Marcus again asked a third time.

"One thing at a time." Jason replied. "First, I want to tell you a story. Today, Tammy and I went out to the auction in North Dover. It was a nice day, and during the auction, I bought the two trunks which are located on the floor for a grand total of twenty-five hundred dollars."

Marcus pivoted his chair to look over the chests and started plucking through the items in them while Jason continued the story. None of the things from the chest looked expensive or collectible, but then again, Marcus wouldn't know if any of the items were worth twenty-five hundred dollars or were collectible. The value or rarity of historical objects was not Marcus' area of specialty. Jason was the historian. Marcus, the anthropologist.

"So, you are saying that these items are worth a lot of money then?" Marcus asked, still browsing the contents of the chests.

"These items?" Jason said, looking at the items on the floor with a slight chuckle. "No, these items are barely worth junk price, and I almost made the same mistake you made looking through them. Look a little closer."

Marcus was a little confused about what Jason was telling him, and Marcus started going through the items a bit more carefully. After a few more moments, Jason could barely contain himself and removed from the top of the first chest underneath the lid's lining an old, weathered envelope.

Jason handed Marcus the envelope. The name *Jessie H. Hillman, Jr.* was written in cursive on the front. "This envelope was found exactly where I just showed you. I almost missed finding the envelope myself." Jason nodded his head as if asking Marcus to open the envelope in front of him to see for himself. On opening the envelope, Marcus thought Jason had cracked. There were three weathered pages yellowed with nothing written on them. Was this the big to-do Jason had rushed him over to see?

"Jason, where is Tammy?" Marcus was almost afraid to ask.

"Oh, Tammy, we had an argument, and she left when she saw what was in the chests. *But I didn't find the envelope until after she left.*" Jason emphasized.

"You don't see it, do you? I have to admit I also gave up and didn't think much about the papers you hold in your hand. Just another disappointment like the chests, I thought, but then by sheer luck, I happened to have been holding the papers close to the fireplace when I made a telephone call asking Tammy to forgive me and come back home." Laughing at himself, Jason continued, "When I looked back at the papers, there was writing on them. Go ahead, try to make the writing appear yourself." Jason prompted.

Marcus stared at his friend Jason in the face. Marcus firmly believed Jason had cracked. What would Jason say to Marcus when no writing appeared on the papers? Marcus swiveled the parlor chair close to the fire and held the three documents before the fire. Sweat perched on Marcus' forehead from the warmth of the fire as the plump man held the papers towards the fire. Then like magic, writing started to appear.

Marcus almost fell out of the chair and had to brace himself on the desk.

"How was this possible?" Marcus asked.

"A child's trick almost. Lemon Juice." Jason replied.

"Lemon Juice?" Marcus repeated.

"You need to brush up on your Edgar Allan Poe." Jason said, smirking. Marcus did not get the reference. Jason continued and pulled up Wikipedia on his computer on the desk. In the query box, he typed the words "Edgar Allan Poe, Gold Bug." And the screen changed to a summary of the short story The Gold Bug, written by Edgar Allan Poe, published in Eighteen Forty-Three. Marcus continued reading the synopsis on Wikipedia while holding the papers in his hands.

The Gold Bug was the story of a treasure hunt, written on a piece of parchment with lemon juice that, when heated, revealed a treasure map off the Carolinas coast. In the story, the bug made of gold was used as a weight. When dropped through the eye of a skull from a specific tree branch would reveal the exact digging location of the treasure.

"You don't mean to tell me that the lemon juice was written on these papers all those years ago and was preserved until you found the envelope just now," Marcus asked.

"Read the letter, judge for yourself, but the acid would act as a natural preservative, especially on the parchment you are holding." Jason stood above him, the shadows catching his unshaven face from the light of the fire.

With the invitation to read the pages, Marcus began reading.

7 - The Letter

Dear Jessie,

Brother, if you are reading this, I have not come home and most likely perished. Unfortunately, then I could not tell you this most important news in person because this news affects the future of all our generations. I have paid the ladies attending me two gold pieces to deliver this letter to you in secret. I trust them to act on my behalf.

I know this message will be delivered safely because you alone will remember how we passed secretive messages to one another as children. If the ladies did open the envelope, they will assuredly be most baffled why I would pay them to send blank pages as my last will and testament.

The war is almost over, Richmond has fallen, and last I heard, Jefferson Davis has fled. While in Richmond recovering from my wounds, I was reassigned to work in a most secretive detail. I and six others, accompanied by a Corporal riding a wagon with four horses, escorted a cache of boxes from Richmond to Texas. We were ordered not to look into the packages we escorted. We were afraid the boxes contained explosives or ammunition to resupply the western front. We set out in the black of night, the seven of us.

The travel was slow going. The men picked for the assignment had already been demoralized injury or from the loss of Richmond. We felt sure surrender would soon happen, and for us fighting men to be going in the opposite direction from the battle and our homes did nothing to satisfy us as southern men. Eventually, curiosity besets the best of men, and some of the men peeked in the ammunition crates without the Corporal seeing them one night. To their surprise, the boxes contained confederate gold bars and coins. Word quickly spread amongst the rest of the group via whispers.

The Corporal could hear the whispers and excitement, but being a man, one man, he could only keep his eyes open for so long as the men around him plotted. Soon after the discovery, the Corporal was laid to rest in a shallow grave. The six of us quickly began counting our fortunes and telling tales of how we should split the gold and set plans for how the gold should be best spent to avoid any questions being asked.

Needless to say, greed is rampant, and arguments amongst us ensued. Three of us sided on venturing to California and starting over under assumed names. The others sided on splitting up the gold and forgetting we ever met. But gold is heavy, and arguments are deadly, and what started as an argument over who should retain the wagon erupted in a knife fight between the leaders of both groups. The knife fight quickly changed to a pistol fight with everyone being killed except me, who took a stab through the abdomen. The wound I endured wasn't a lethal one, but nonetheless, I did come out bloodied but victorious.

Killing those other men was not my proudest moment on this planet. God forgive me. But there is no talking someone out of trying to kill you when the prospect of a fortune is involved. I grabbed my shotgun, and with the horses attached to the wagon and gold in hand, started west. I had no plan and truthfully still don't. Eventually, exhausted from my wound and fatigue, I passed out. When I awoke, I was in the middle of nowhere, a long stretch of land with no trees or weeds to be seen, but I was on a road. So, I followed the road for what seemed to be hours in the baking heat. Then I came to a plantation. I hid the wagon in the woods and observed slaves and overseers working the land. On my right was a rather large lake with a stream leading off to the distance.

Hiding the gold, I untied the horses and, taking one horse, rode to the house where once again I promptly passed out in the presence of three ladies. I do not know how much time I was asleep, and I have feigned fatigue and sleep more than I should have. Still, I could overhear the ladies whispering amongst themselves that infection has gotten into my wound. The sweats and terrors I currently have will only worsen, and I may not recover.

34

That night, I went downstairs undetected and am writing this letter to you. Tomorrow, I will ask them to deliver this letter to you in the event I cannot tell you in person about the gold, which should now go to our family. It is of the utmost importance that I should not perish for nothing but rather create a legacy for our family if I should die.

The ladies themselves are being terrorized by the men left to watch over the slaves of the plantation. I hear them being brutalized by the ogres but am too weak to defend them. The women have no choice but to leave soon as their hopes of their men returning had faded when I informed them of the fate of Richmond. I will ask them to deliver this letter upon my death when they leave.

Tell no one of this as greed will overcome all who hear of this. The plantation is located in Walnford County, Mississippi. I have drawn a crude map and have faith in you.

God Speed,

Your brother,

Robert A. Hillman, Jr.
1865

8 – Jason Matthews

"Eighteen sixty-five?" Marcus said almost to himself but out loud.

"One hundred and fifty-six years ago." Jason said.
"This is a treasure map." Marcus said, staring at the last page. The map was a semi-detailed drawing of the plantation. The lake was visible in the center of the crude drawing. The woods and crops, the main house, servant's house, icehouse, barns, and many smaller structures were visible.

"That was my opinion as well. Like I said, an opportunity of a lifetime." Jason said.

"You don't believe in all this, do you?" Marcus asked.

"Why not. Think about the scenario like this, for one hundred and fifty years, confederate gold has been buried on a plantation somewhere, and no one knows where. Now we do. Fact number one, we know as historians that no large caches of confederate gold have ever been found following the civil war. But we know for a fact the confederates had access to gold and were starting to mint gold coins for currency. They also wanted to make payments to France to enter the war on the south's behalf. Fact number two, we as a society know there are large sums of gold that have never been recovered hidden from the civil war. Fact three and most indisputably we have here evidence of where that gold is being hidden." Jason said in the affirmative.

"You are forgetting one thing we don't *really* know where the gold is. There is no place on the map indicating a location. No X marks the spot, so to speak." Marcus said, arguing.

Jason sat across from Marcus on the other side of the desk, "I noticed the same thing." Jason said, reaching across the desk, grabbing a bottle of brandy and two small glasses from the beverage cart, and removing the stopper, poured the brandy into the two small glasses. He passed one of the glasses to Marcus.

"There are a lot of problems with the map and letter, sure we have a state and a name for an old farm, but no exact location on the gold. For all, we know there is a shopping plaza built on top of the old farmhouse location, and the gold was removed long ago. But if the gold is there, this..." Jason said, holding his glass up to the light, "This is an opportunity of a lifetime, and I need a partner. Marcus, will you be my partner?"

"What exactly does a partnership entitle me to?" Marcus asked as he swallowed the brandy in one gulp and sat back to feel the fire on the back of his neck.

"I need a partner for several reasons. One Gold is heavy. Logistically, I cannot carry that much gold by myself. No man could. Two, a lot of research on Walnford Plantation will need to be done, research on the Hillman family, what became of them and their family. Lastly, we'll need to think about where the gold could be *before* we get there. The drive and trip to drive to Mississippi is roughly a day. We need to have a plan mapped out about where the most likely places are the gold could be hidden. We can't just arrive there and start digging. Anyone passing by would be way too curious about the reason we are there, and it would be way too hard to explain to the local authorities why we are there."

"So, how about one-third percent of any recoveries?" Jason said, finishing his brandy.

"We'll need to agree first, we aren't doing this to get famous, and we are partnering to get rich. Go big or go home." Marcus said.

"I agree no historical documentaries, articles, or books based on this event. Purely based on avarice. Go big or go home." Jason said with a smile.

"Are you in?" Jason asked after a brief pause.
"Yea, Yea. I'm in." Marcus said, returning the smile.

"Of course, we can't tell anyone about this." Jason said.
"I agree. What will you tell Tammy?" Marcus asked.

"She'll come with us. I know that when I tell her about this, she will be excited to come with us. Besides, we'll need a third person to help carry all the equipment and hopefully all that gold." Jason said, pouring himself another brandy.

"Do you think that's wise? Telling your wife, I mean?" Marcus said.

"Marcus, I trust my wife completely with everything I hold dear, including my life." Jason said.

"So, where do we start?" Marcus asked.

"Where all good research begins, my dear Watson, the library." Jason said.

9 – Dominic Cross

"I want you to kill my husband." The words hung in the air as the couple lay in bed.

Dominic took these words as an insult. What Tammy finally revealed with the sentence was what Tammy honestly thought of Dominic. Disposable, someone to be used and discarded, Dominic thought. Not just him, he thought, but all men, her husband too. There was no shock, no questions, no entertaining the thought of killing her husband. Cross ignored the request. Dominic knew what this was, a fling and nothing more. Her using him, this request didn't make the end of their relationship hurt any less, but Dominic always knew the ending of their affair would come to this. Maybe not in this way, but with them separating and someone getting hurt. Separating from one another was bound to happen eventually.

Maybe there was surprise or something else entirely, but Tammy didn't ask a second time for Dominic to kill her husband, and there was no further discussion of killing her husband that night. Dominic rolled over onto his back, and Tammy slept quietly on his chest. Was she sleeping? He couldn't be sure, and he didn't want to move and ruin this moment. There was just too much playing in his mind now. Was she awake or dreaming? Dominic was confident that whatever they had shared physically between them was now over. But the hurt feelings would not leave Dominic's head.

After a night of laying in the dark, with their naked body's entangled with one another, morning came. And with morning, a knock came on the door. Dominic putting his jeans on, answered the door as Tammy lay in the bed. At the door stood a six-foot-seven tall man Dominic knew as "Scooter." Scooter's real name was

Alex. No last name. No one ever called him Alex, just Scooter. He was a slim man, tattoo sleeves on both arms and a pointy black beard with a bandana. Your prototypical biker, one would think. What else could he be? With a name like Scooter, Dominic thought.

Scooter like Dominic was a member of the Nomad Motorcycle club. A few weeks before Dominic, he was released from prison after serving an eight and half year sentence for murder and winning an appeal for ineffective counsel. Both Scooter and Dominic had been told the same thing upon release, the Nomads were happy they were out of jail, but the club was too hot right now.

As Cross learned, one of their associates purchased weapons from an undercover Alcohol, Tobacco, and Firearms agent in a converted car with a hidden compartment for transporting firearms or narcotics. The Nomads utilized this source and his vehicle for several transactions only to have Federal agents raid their area clubs simultaneously. The transporter with the car was an undercover officer. As a result, many brother Nomads would be doing some time. If Dominic and Scooter showed up, interacting with those under indictment, it could violate the terms of their parole immediately. When everything had blown over at the club, an invitation to come home would be sent, but for now, there was no telling how long that invitation could be. In the meantime, the message was to stay clear.

Behind Scooter was Melinda, a much shorter woman than Scooter and even smaller than Tammy, but not in Tammy's physical shape. Melinda had junk in the trunk, as the saying went, and she belonged to Scooter. When Scooter was sent to prison initially, the sentence was considered life; thirty years. The Nomads had Melinda marry Scooter as a symbol of moral support. She belonged to the club, and the club offered Melinda to Scooter while he was incarcerated to show Scooter support. Only after eight and half years, the unthinkable had happened, Scooter won his appeal and his freedom.

Both Scooter and Melinda stood at the door, not realizing Dominic wasn't alone. Dominic waved them both into the room and shut the door behind them. Scooter at eight-thirty in the morning already had a beer bottle in his hand.

"Scooter, Melinda, meet Tammy. She wants us to murder her husband for her." Dominic said point-blank.

Before Tammy could object or say otherwise, Dominic threw Tammy her clothes and told her to get dressed. Tammy took the clothes Dominic had thrown her and the blanket from the bed, covering herself as she ran to the bathroom to get dressed.

Scooter gave Dominic an approving look at his choice of females and their anatomy before being smacked in the stomach by Melinda. Melinda sat on the bed while Dominic and Scooter sat opposite one other at the table next to the door. Then, the toilet flushed, and Tammy appeared from the bathroom.

"I don't know what you are talking about. Murdering my husband." Tammy started to say before being cut off.

"Tammy, this is my family, Scooter and Melinda. They are part of the same..." Dominic searched for the proper word. "Family as me. If you want me to kill your husband, you are asking all of us. Comprende?" Dominic said.

"Now, let's talk turkey. This..." Dominic said, pointing between himself and Tammy, "Has been a shitload of fun, but we both knew the sex wasn't going to last forever. Frankly, I'm glad you're giving me an out with a financial incentive so let's talk numbers. How much are we talking to kill off your husband?"

Tammy paused briefly before answering. "How about fifteen thousand dollars. My husband has a life insurance policy through the University, where he works for one hundred thousand dollars. It could take some time to get the money, though." She said.

Scooter leaned over and whispered in Dominic's ear.

"My associate here doesn't think fifteen thousand is enough. He is a professional who has killed people. He says a murder like this would cost you twenty-five thousand upfront in cash." Dominic said.

She was thinking and thinking hard, Dominic thought. Cross didn't like when women pondered something because he knew women were always smarter than men. If Tammy was thinking about something, there was a reason. He just couldn't put his finger on what she was thinking about.

"I can't come up with twenty-five. Can we meet in the middle and consider an even twenty? Also, if I give you twenty thousand upfront, how would I be sure you just wouldn't pick up and leave and not do the job? I think things would be only fair if I was to pay you half up front and the other half after the job was done." Tammy said.

41

There was more whispering between Scooter and Dominic, this time though Tammy said to Scooter, "Anything you have to say to him, you can say to me. I am right here."

"I like her. She has balls." Said Melinda referring to Tammy as she sat watching and listening.

Dominic said. "Okay. Twenty thousand, but you don't come back here again, someone could see us together and then next thing you know they start talking to the police. Another thing, you don't call the hotel or me on your cell phone. Use a payphone. If you can't find a payphone, use a business line in the mall or a shop. In fact, lose your phone altogether, those things have GPS units inside, and if they track the phone, the cellular signal will lead the authorities right here back to us at this meeting. So, lose the phone. When you have the ten thousand dollars, we'll discuss the specifics of how and when we'll take care of business. Any questions?"

Tammy stood up and grabbed her purse and sunglasses. She gave Dominic a hug. The hug was more a symbolic gesture than a symbol of any lingering feelings removed from their relationship. Their relationship was defined and made clear now. This was a business relationship. Anything physical between Dominic and Tammy was now gone.

After Tammy left the motel, Dominic, Scooter, and Melinda sat outside on a picnic table under a tree eating some Subway sandwiches from across the street. As usual, the money the Nomads had sent for the month would just barely cover the rent and some food. Therefore, twenty thousand was a lot of money when you had none. Twenty thousand dollars was months of money to live with on the road. The conversation on how to commit the murder was surprisingly simple.

"After she pays us the ten thousand, the day we do the job, we check out of the motel that morning and leave town. We send Melinda back in about two weeks to make sure she pays us the other ten. How the job gets done, the specifics, none of the details matter, either running him over with a car or shooting him he won't see us coming." Dominic said.

"She should pay us the whole thing upfront. I don't like hanging around a murder scene waiting to get paid." Scooter said.

"Once she pays us the ten thousand, we can always renegotiate the deal at that time. Try to get more upfront. It's not like she can go to her husband or the police." They all nodded their heads in agreement with the thought blackmail could potentially work.

"As far as committing the murder, Tammy will be able to tell us when her husband is most vulnerable and when she has the best chance at an alibi. Let her work out the details. Any other thoughts on the subject?" Dominic said, asking the others.

"Yea. Don't miss." Melinda said as she turned her hand into a fake gun and pointed her index finger at Dominic, and made a "pew" sound like she was firing a gun. The table erupted with a burst of laughter, and Dominic reflected on that statement while he drank his soda. Don't miss, he thought. She had a point.

10 – Abrams

Abrams started his investigation of the missing Marc and Stacey Harden by making telephone calls to the family members, friends, and co-workers. These telephone calls often accomplished one or two objectives, either raising further concern among those already worried or the calls showed that someone was taking an interest in their loved one's lives and subsequent disappearance. Very infrequently did the telephone interviews reveal any new details not already known previously by the family. This call was based more on the second objective. Someone was taking an interest in their loved one's affairs.

Most telephone calls to parents, siblings, co-workers, or friends led essentially nowhere with the same information already established being rehashed. Most knew Stacey and Mark were traveling to Tennessee to visit a sick relative. There was a definitive return timeline as neither Marc nor Stacey expected to be gone longer than a week. Calls to employers revealed both Marc and Stacey should have returned to work by now. With nothing new learned from the telephone calls, Abrams went with his next lead, Brooke Mueller.

Abrams met Brooke at her sister's house, and together they would do a once over of the place to look for any indicators Brooke may have missed during her search of the residence previously. Both starting searching in the kitchen, going through the trash and bathrooms, working their way into the living room.

"What is the percentage of people who are found after being declared missing?" Brooke asked Abrams.

Abrams was going through a stack of letters and envelopes, answered, "Everything depends on the circumstances. If the missing was a child, we could certainly call this an abduction, and the chances of having that child returned alive are about one in twenty thousand. Since these are adults, our chances are a little better. Statistics are about one in about every three hundred. But, if we believe these adults may not want to be found and left on their own, our chances may get much better than that, say one in about one hundred." Abrams was staring at a checkbook with a healthy balance of over fifteen thousand in joint savings.

Brooke walked across the room wearing a pair of heels and yoga pants covered by a white sweater with buttons. Her long brunette hair was pinned back in a ponytail. She then knelt on the floor and started going through a chest of papers while Abrams went through the nearby desk drawers. However, his attention was thoroughly captivated when he looked over to see what Brooke was doing and was staring at Brooke's pink thong underwear while she was bent over.

Abrams couldn't help but stare at Brooke's ass. Was Brooke bending over in front of him on purpose, Abrams asked himself? She had to know what she was doing bending over in front of him like that, he thought to himself. Doubt crept into Abrams' mind, and he turned away, ashamed. But then he looked back again and wished he was ten or twenty years younger. He sighed.

"I think I'm going to take a look around upstairs." Abrams said, watching Brooke's backside as he walked up the landing.

"A waste of time." Brooke said about an hour later the when the search was over, and nothing of significance was found.

"Not necessarily. I think we can effectively rule out that Marc and Stacey took an extended trip on purpose. The trash can was still full. The food in the refrigerator would expire in a few days, and on their desk by the checkbook were several bills which have just come past due. Very odd for a couple with over fifteen thousand dollars to deliberately not pay their cable bill on time, wouldn't you say?" Abrams asked rhetorically.

"So, searching here wasn't pointless. We were able to eliminate a possibility. Unfortunately, that leaves some very unpleasant possibilities." Abrams said.

"Like what?" Brooke asked.

"That something or someone bad happened upon them." Abrams said as he got into his car. "Tomorrow, I broaden the

45

search. I'll be in touch when I have some news. Good night Ms. Mueller." Abrams said as he drove away.

That night drinking his bourbon and watching television, unable to sleep, Abrams thought about Brooke Mueller. Was there a possibility Brooke purposefully knew what she was doing wearing and exposing her pink thong back at the Harden's residence? Was Abrams just being obsessive? Not a bad problem to have for sure, just something to keep an eye on. Nothing worse than misreading a situation and reacting to biased, inappropriate sexual interests. Brooke came to Abrams for help. He would not want to lose all sense of professionalism while she was vulnerable or not interested. Everything could be ruined or predicated on a poor, hastily made decision, he thought as he fell asleep in his recliner.

The following day the real private detective work began. Which was not as exciting as in the movies. In this case, Abrams felt; option one was to search the internet and find every police department between Texas and Tennessee and their bordering states, Alabama, Mississippi, and Arkansas. The work to call the police departments could become very time-consuming. Scouring the internet, then finding and calling precincts in the local municipalities. Abrams was aware of the procedures and the departments' priority on outside callers not working for the Texas State Police. Once someone picked up the phone at the police department, they would undoubtedly transfer him to a detective or an impound yard. Which would probably go unanswered straight to voice mail. More than half of those who received those messages would never call him back.

Not a very appealing option. Which left a second option. Brooke had provided a copy of Marc and Stacey's car registration which listed the year, license, make, and model of their vehicle. Something any tow truck company keeping a car in their lot could easily track. Most tow truck companies kept a computerized list because their company would charge a tow fee plus an automatic fifteen to twenty-five dollars a day the vehicle was stored. Any company not looking to obtain these amounts would seemingly never want to be paid. If calling tow truck companies did not pan out, Abrams thought calls to individual hospitals would need to be made.

The problem with this second option was the same as number one but not nearly as bad. Abrams would need to create lists of tow truck companies by state from Texas to Tennessee and their surrounding counties. Suppose there were twenty to thirty tow truck companies per county in any given state. In that case, he could conservatively be looking at anywhere near fifteen hundred calls when he was finished after the list was completed. A very daunting task for one person to undertake.

He didn't think Marc and Stacey had disappeared in Texas. Call this thought a hunch, but having this couple disappear so close to home just didn't sound right to him. He would call the Texas tow truck companies last if he needed to, he decided. So, Abrams started in the internet yellow pages in Tennessee. Abrams stopped after six hours of placing calls and eliminating tow truck companies. There was no sign of the vehicle Marc and Stacey had driven anywhere in Tennessee. The next day he chose to call Arkansas; before calling this time, Abrams could eliminate as a guess the state's northern counties. The thinking was Marc and Stacey would not detour too far from their destination in Tennessee. He could come back if he needed to, he thought, but hopefully not.

On the third day of calls, Abrams struck pay dirt. Walnford County, located in the northwest most section of Mississippi. The car lot belonged to Advanced One Towing, and the gentleman on the other end said the car had been there for just under two weeks. After Abrams jotted down the address for the towing lot, he map-quested the directions, just over seven hours of driving. Out of curiosity or perhaps habit, he looked the area of Tunica up on google. Sixth largest Casino area in the United States with nine casino resorts. Not a very populated place, but according to Wikipedia, several ghost towns were listed nearby. Walnford County was also very close to several major connecting highways. This lead felt right. The county sat close to resort destinations and the Mississippi River with large plots of unpopulated areas.

First thing pre-dawn, he would leave and head straight for Walnford County and the Advanced One towing lot. If he lucked out, he would be there by two in the afternoon. No sense in calling Brooke, although he wanted to. If the lead on her sister turned out to not be the missing car, this misinformation could only further upset Brooke. Best to update her once he had eyes on the vehicle. But for the rest of tonight, after three days of making phone calls, he thought a little celebration was in order opening his desk and taking the whiskey bottle out.

11 - Jason Matthews

Jason Matthews and Marcus Robertson started their search the next day at the university library. But, before heading over to the university library to look for information, Tammy Matthews had returned home in the morning. Tammy's face visually showed somewhere between unhappiness and contempt at seeing Marcus at the house early in the morning. Upon arriving home, her husband told Tammy of the events from the proceeding night. After a period of disbelief, she saw the reappearing ink working and how the designs on the map came up when held to a heat source. Much to Jason's surprise, Tammy's anger had turned to enthusiasm. This enthusiasm was once again short-lived and turned to rage when Jason told Tammy Marcus was now a one-third partner in their search for gold.

After a row of morning apologies and hugs, Jason told Tammy, Marcus, and he would be going to the university's library to search for information on Walnford Plantation, the Hillman family, and clues to where the gold may be hidden and what is on the land now. Tammy suggested making a copy of the map when it was heated. Avoiding having to heat the map every time the map needed to be used. An excellent idea, voiced Jason as he and Marcus left the house for the library.

"I get the distinct feeling she hates me. Did you see her face? She barely acknowledged me. I think she wanted to kill me, or you may be in reverse order when you told her I was a one-third partner." As Jason and Marcus got in Marcus' car and started driving, Marcus said.

"Nonsense. Tammy barely knows you, that's all." Jason said.

"I wish I could be more confident about that." Marcus said, trying to relax while driving.

"I've been thinking. We need a plan on how to maximize our focus, energy, and time when we go to the library." Jason said.

"Any ideas?" Marcus asked.

"A few let me know what you think. I can start in the microfilm room looking at newspaper articles from Mississippi around eighteen sixty-five if they have them. If you can start the genealogy and history searches, books, magazines, we may be able to work much faster." Jason said.

"I think this is going to be much more than one trip and a one-day search. This could be several days of digging through archives, and we still might be missing stuff that is local or regional to Mississippi. If anything is cataloged which the university doesn't have, we may have to order the periodical."

Once at the library, the two split up, promising to meet for lunch at the university cafeteria at one. The going was slow and tedious for Jason. Going to the librarian and asking for any microfilm regarding Mississippi circa eighteen sixty-five. At first, Jason didn't think there would be much the university would have in terms of newspapers on microfilm from that period. However, the librarian brought out three microfilm trays with countless rolls of microfilm.

The older librarian said, "I brought you out eighteen sixty-four and eighteen sixty-six as well. Just in case you needed them."

"If your search was after nineteen twenty, these would all be available on the computer, but I'm afraid there is no real interest in having anyone put these onto a modern hard drive. A shame." She said, handing off the tray of microfilm.

Jason thanked her and, seated at the microfilm station, carefully placed the microfilm into the case and placed his hand on the roller ball to scroll through the headlines. Eighteen sixty-four was a bust. There were many articles regarding the ongoing war, both from a national perspective and a local view. Some smaller newspapers had written articles about the damage the northerners were doing or a local boy who became a hero by fighting off a Yankee patrol by himself. A few articles regarding some plantations contributing to the war effort but nothing specifically about the Walnford Plantation. Also, nothing about the gold, the hillman family, or the Walnford family.

During this time, Jason got the idea to call over to Mississippi University to gather information from a local historian from the area that may shed some light on the Walnford Plantation or the Walnford family and could be a much quicker way to gain information. Jason decided he would need to discuss the idea with Marcus before making the call. The idea of having anyone else inquiring or knowing about something as remote as this could bring more questions than Jason was prepared to answer.

His cell phone indicated the time was just after eleven. Two more hours until he could take a break. He set back working at the microfilm, and in March eighteen, sixty-five stories began to talk of the desperate hours of Richmond and the plight of the southern family should the North win the war. One newspaper article detailed a letter from Robert E. Lee to Jefferson Davis to evacuate Richmond with haste. Jefferson Davis set all paperwork on fire and quickly abandoned the city.

Would that be about the same time the patrol escorting the cache of gold was told to head west? The dates would match and make sense. This could add further validity to the letter being authentic. Pressing on, Jason kept scrolling through the headlines of microfilm. Finally, after Appomattox Courthouse in June eighteen sixty-five, a smaller newspaper, the Glendale Register-Herald, listed six pages of Mississippi men who had not yet returned from fighting in the war and assumed dead. Listed on page three are Jacob Walnford Sr., Jacob Walnford Jr., and Christopher Walnford.

A quick internet search for the Glendale Register-Herald revealed the paper was now a defunct newspaper. Glendale was located in Alcorn, Mississippi, which had gone on to become just Glen, Mississippi. According to Google, the town now only had two hundred and eighty-six residents. The chief business of the area was now the Kingsford Charcoal plant. Was Walnford plantation located in Alcorn County? Jason asked himself.

Nearing on one in the afternoon, he asked the local librarian to hold the rest of the microfilm for him until he returned from lunch.

Jason was the first to arrive outside the University cafeteria. The cafeteria itself segregated the faculty and students. However, many of the faculty still did not take the opportunity of eating at the cafeteria. The feeling that many faculty felt they were above eating there was very prevalent. After waiting no longer than five minutes, Marcus appeared. The two quickly moving through the buffet line and finding plenty of empty seats to talk amongst themselves privately.

After sitting down, Jason found himself ravenously hungry and began eating when Marcus asked him how the search was going.

"Very slow, I am afraid. I started with the Microfilm in eighteen sixty-four through eighteen sixty-six. I am only halfway through currently. I may be able to finish up a cursory look this afternoon." Digging into his satchel, Jason produced a handful of pages he had printed from the Microfilm and turned them over to Marcus.

"Richmond fell in eighteen sixty-five. Jefferson Davis received a secret dispatch from Robert E. Lee informing Jefferson of Grant's arrival in Richmond and telling him to vacate the city. This article would seem to validate the timeline for the letter. With the gold possibly being transported out of the city in anticipation of the arrival of the Union. Then there was this taken from the Glendale Register-Herald, a list of names of missing soldiers who never returned from the war and were considered missing. On the list were three Walnford family members, Jacob Sr., Jacob Jr., and Christopher Walnford. "So, would it be so far-fetched to believe that Walnford plantation is located in Alcorn County near Glendale?" Jason proposed.

"Walnford Plantation is not located in Alcorn county at all. It's in Walnford county. It's a smaller subsection of Tunica." Marcus said with a smile.

12 – Tammy Matthews

When Tammy left the impromptu meeting in the morning after her last physical night with Dominic Cross, Tammy Matthews felt disgusted. She was not disgusted by the physical act of sex with Dominic, which she always enjoyed, but of how Tammy felt when she asked Dominic Cross to murder her husband. In Tammy's mind, she had the upper hand and had planned on a smooth scenario she could control. Scooter and Melinda being invited into the planning stages of the murder directly implicated, this giving up her leverage. Scooter and Melinda could end up serving as potential witnesses against her in the event they were caught.

Scooter and Melinda were now wild cards. The more people involved in this murder, the greater chances Tammy had of getting caught, she felt. Of all the thoughts about what could now go wrong with the plan to murder her husband, Tammy hadn't counted on Dominic inviting other people into a murder conspiracy. Tammy had every intention of double-crossing Dominic after the murder was committed. She was even smart enough to lie about how much money the life insurance from the university would be coming her way. One hundred thousand was a low-ball figure Tammy had come up with. She fully expected an initial counteroffer after offering fifteen thousand. However, she couldn't believe how cheap life was to these people when they had accepted the twenty thousand.

Now, she would be double-crossing three people and her husband. She had no intentions of paying Dominic Cross anything. But the prospect of getting rid of two additional people who would undoubtedly try shaking her down or blackmail her for more money after the murder would prove more troublesome. She thought about this as she arrived home to find Marcus Robertson's car in the driveway. As Tammy entered the house, she discovered her husband Jason and Marcus getting ready to leave for the day.

Upon arriving home, Jason invited her to come upstairs, with Marcus following. Jason was rambling; he kept on apologizing for his behavior the night before. Jason didn't ask where she had spent the night. He just kept asking her to come upstairs. Jason was acting mysterious, as if he was hiding something, sneaking about. When she arrived upstairs, with Marcus Robertson behind her, Jason began talking.

"I have something to show you. Something that was in the chests we bought at the auction." Jason said.

With that, Jason handed Tammy the blank pieces of paper. Like Marcus the night before, she also thought Jason had cracked when he had given her three blank pages. Jason then prepared the fireplace in his office and took the papers from Tammy, showing her the writing which appeared when heated. Tammy couldn't believe her eyes. The words and map appearing on the parchment were like a magic trick.

When she read the papers about the confederate gold and the location, she read the letter a second time. Mouthing each word as she read the letter silently to herself. A treasure map containing confederate gold. Was this for real? Before she could ask Jason, he was already answering her.

"Pretty unbelievable stuff?" Jason asked her as Tammy hugged him and wrapped her arms around his waist, beginning to cry.

"Now, now don't cry. There is nothing to cry about. This is all good news. Marcus and I and you will all be very wealthy if this turns out to be true and the gold is waiting for us at Walnford Plantation." Jason said.

"Wait, Marcus?" Tammy asked.
"Yes, he's our business partner in this adventure now. A full one-third partner." Jason said.

"One-third? Jason, you can't be serious. These are our chests and our map. This is our gold. What has he contributed?" Tammy asked, temporarily forgetting Marcus was standing in the office's doorway listening to the exchange between husband and wife.

Jason took her hands, the letter and map from her, said, "We need him more than you know. He will help us find the location. Right now, we have a name of a plantation. Additionally, let's say we do find the gold. Is the gold buried? Does recovering the gold require a lot of digging? Moving gold is also very laborious. Way too heavy for just two people to carry, and lift a third person would be advantageous. Lastly, Marcus has offered to fund all the tools we will need for our expedition. His loss will be almost equivalent to our own should this search prove pointless. Now, what do you say?"

For a moment, the second time that morning, Tammy changed her mood from mad or upset to suddenly manageable. An inkling of a plan was developing in the corner of Tammy's mind. The first time she had this inkling was earlier in the morning when she had low-balled Dominic Cross to murder her husband with a twenty-thousand-dollar offer. Marcus's help was not precisely what Tammy was thinking about, but she needed to play along for the crowd around her. Jason recognized the reversal in her effect.

"Everything makes sense now. We'll need all the help we can get, and Marcus is someone we can trust." Tammy said, changing her tune to fit her husband's perceptions.

"Exactly. Marcus and I were just heading to the university library to research the letter and map and see if we could pinpoint where the gold may be hidden or if the gold is still there? Would you like to come with us? We could use the help." Jason replied excited Tammy had seen things his way.

"No. No. You two go ahead and remember to make a copy of the map when the map is heated, so we don't have to keep warming it up to read." Tammy said. With the conversation ended and a kiss on the cheek, both Jason and Marcus left. Tammy went downstairs and got into a hot shower and again thought she had everything figured out. As Tammy showered, the details of the murder conspiracy began taking shape in her mind.

After taking her shower and getting changed, Tammy believed she had pieced together a plot to murder her husband. Driving to a local hotel, she asked the concierge to use the telephone for a local call. The clerk placed the phone on the counter and walked to the other side of the lobby to provide Tammy some privacy. Tammy dialed the hotel phone number for Dominic Cross and asked the receptionist to connect her call to room twelve.

Cross picked up on the third ring. "That was quick. Having second thoughts?" Cross said without asking who was on the other end of the phone.

"No second thoughts. But you won't believe what I have to tell you." Tammy said.

"Go ahead, make me a believer then." Cross said, being playful.

"How about instead of insurance money like we talked about, you get paid in gold bars?"

"How much are we talking about?" Cross asked, now laughing.

"Millions." She said enticingly.

"Yea, right, and I am supposed to believe you have stacks of gold bars lying around, I suppose." Dominic said as he lay in the bed unconvinced.

"It's true. You are just going to have to work a little harder to get paid, and you could be set for life." Tammy replied.

"Sounds like you are up to something. Nothing is ever as good as it seems. Tell me more." Cross said.

"This morning, when I came home, my husband found a map leading to lost confederate gold. This could be worth millions if the gold is still there. They're at the university library researching the map they found now."

"Lost confederate gold? You are pulling my leg, right?" Cross asked.

"No, I'm not making this up. We will be taking a little trip in a few days or weeks to go and get gold. You could follow us, and when we get there, have them get the gold. You get rid of them and let me keep the full amount of life insurance." Tammy said.

"Millions of dollars at stake, and all you want is your measly one hundred thousand? That doesn't make any sense." Cross said.

"Well, things are a little more complicated now. There's a partner who is traveling with us. His friend Marcus Robertson. He's not much to be concerned about, a fat greasy bald man. But he's an issue you will need to clean up as well." Tammy said.

"Let me get this straight. These two have a treasure map to millions in lost gold. Why would we not just take the map and letter off them now?" Cross said.

"Several reasons, first the map is not an exact location of where the gold is buried. You need them to figure out where the gold is and maybe even get it for you. Lastly, killing them out of state gives me an alibi. Even though I will be traveling with them, I can say they never came back, and when they are found dead, I will have an alibi." Tammy said. That part about an alibi was bullshit Tammy thought, but would Cross buy her bullshit was the question?

"Alright. I'm starting to like this plan." Cross said.
"I told you I would come up with one. This just fell into my lap this morning. Two professors go for a ride and get carjacked or robbed and are found dead several hours away. Could happen to anyone." Tammy said.

"I like the part where they will show us where the gold is and maybe dig their graves while digging up the gold. How confident are you about the gold being there?" Cross asked still hesitant.

"Maybe fifty-fifty it's there, fifty-fifty it's not. The map and letter were real. I held the papers in my hands this morning. But one hundred and fifty years is a long time for someone not to come along and find the gold by accident." Tammy said.

"If the gold's not there, then what?" Cross asked.

"Then we stick to our original agreement. Twenty thousand, but I don't want to hear about any upfront payments. If this happens and the gold is there, you are going to be extremely rich." Tammy said.

The phone went silent on the other end. Cross was still mulling things through, thinking everything presented to him over.

"I'll have to talk to the others first. Call me back tomorrow." Cross said after a long pause.

"No problem. But you'll need to be ready to move in a few days. I may not be able to give you much notice if we need to move right away." Tammy said.

"Alright. I'll talk to you tomorrow." Cross said, and the end of the line went dead.

Hanging up the phone, Tammy was pleasantly surprised how well the call went. This had all come together rather nicely. She had no interest in the treasure and doubted the gold even existed. But the opportunity to have everything line up neatly out of state and away from Georgia may be too much to pass up. Thinking like a chess player, she would need to consider variables while trying to stay two steps ahead of both her husband and Dominic Cross. She would need to put the next stage of plans into motion, and Tammy knew she would not have much time.

13 - Marcus Robertson

"Walnford Plantation is in Tunica County, well technically Walnford County." Robertson repeated.

"The Casino town?" Jason asked, then stared at his friend, waiting for Marcus to explain further.

"The first thing I did in my search this morning is to try and attempt to disprove the validity of the letter and the existence of the gold. So, I started with a simple Google search, and I found a recent article by *Sarah Pruitt, Chasing the Myth of Confederate Gold*. In her article, Pruitt corroborates the story of Robert E. Lee sending a dispatch to Jefferson Davis before the fall of Richmond, telling Davis to evacuate the city due to the incoming Union invasion. In response, Davis allegedly put forth two trains filled with gold, sending one north and the second one south." Marcus began.

"It's this part of the story which got me thinking. If you were in charge of a large amount of gold, would you send the entire amount in two trains knowing the Union was destroying train supply lines and could capture the entire haul, essentially putting you out of business? Additionally, both sides employed large networks of spies. These spies would have been watching the train lines waiting to sell this information to the Union. Knowing this as assuredly as Davis probably would, would you still put the gold on the trains?" Marcus asked rhetorically.

"Anyhow, let me continue. Speculation aside, despite putting all the gold on two trains, millions in gold go missing. An exact amount of how much gold went missing is debatable. Various accounts estimate anywhere between two and twenty million. But those are eighteen-fifty values. This could easily have gone up twenty times or more in today's gold values." Marcus stated.

"I agree to put all your eggs, so to speak, in one basket with the trains could be careless. But without validation of any stories of gold being shipped via wagon. This still amounts to just a hypothesis." Jason Matthews said.

"My second search for information was on Walnford plantation. There were very few results, and the results that did appear in the internet search box I was almost ready to discount. I thought they were mistakes or just plain bad URLs." Marcus continued.

"For example, the first search result was on earthquakes in history. Ask yourself, what could earthquakes possibly have to do with a plantation? An earthquake registered an estimated eight point six along the Mississippi River and Tennessee in eighteen-eleven. The earthquake was such a big event in that part of the territory, in eighteen fifty-five, there was a newspaper article in the Mississippi Frontier following up on the damage of the earthquake forty-five years later." Marcus said

"From that article, and I quote, "*The foundation had split open into a seam on the wall creating an underground cavern, some twenty or thirty feet under the ground. It is not known how far back these caverns extend."* There is even a picture included for our viewing pleasure. "Marcus said, showing Jason the image of a man standing in a cellar next to an open crack in the foundation of the wall and ground.

"Remember the photograph was invented in eighteen twenty-nine. To send a photographer and his camera to take a picture of a crack in a wall this long ago was nothing short of amazing back then. Can you guess where the building was with the crack in the wall?" Marcus asked playfully.

"Walnford Plantation, in the main living house." Marcus answered, sliding the picture of the crack in the wall and the article over for Jason to view.

Looking at the black and white photo from the newspaper, the crack in the foundation wall appeared to be over six feet tall. In the picture stood an unidentified man with a hat standing next to an opening in the wall. The seam appeared to be a foot or so larger than him. According to the article, the entrance into the underground cavern was between two and three feet wide. The interior size of the cavern was described as immense with no further details.

"The next search result was a simple online review of a restaurant. According to Google, the review for this restaurant doesn't exist other than in this one online review. The restaurant simply does not exist." Marcus said, reading from the online review, "*Located on a good and secluded road adjacent to old Walnford Plantation off of route seventy-two, it would be easy to overlook Speedy's restaurant and general store. But Speedy's is a great location for truckers to get some peace and enjoy some good food before setting back on the road. Highly recommended.*" Marcus said, reading the google restaurant review.

Again, Marcus passed a copy of the online review over to Jason, who looked at it with great interest.

"Next, I started a Google Earth search off route seventy-two, and this search took several hours and several hundred if not a thousand web pages of google earth. As you know, Google Earth employs aerial imagery combined with 3D imagery to give users an actual street view from satellites above. Because I was looking for a street, I had to look at any streets which were physically connected to route seventy-two and see where they lead to and go through a process of elimination." Marcus continued.

At this time, Marcus passed a Google Earth aerial photo of a building with one car parked outside and what appeared to be a giant sign. "I believe this is the image of Speedy's restaurant and general good store." Marcus said, pointing to an image of a building which sat alone in alone among a deserted road.

The picture had one decaying road across the center of the photo. The building looked like it was built in the late nineteen sixties or early seventies. It was a very cookie-cutter model type building and resembled a townhouse instead of a restaurant. There was no vegetation in the photo, no trees, no shrubbery, and no grass. The building known as Speedy's restaurant would have appeared abandoned if it wasn't for the white pick-up truck parked outside around the back of the restaurant. Dirt and brown overgrown reeds appeared at the outset of the picture.

"I don't know. It almost looks abandoned. We can't tell from this picture if this is Speedy's restaurant or somebody's house." Jason said.

"I thought you might say that. What else do you notice about the picture?" Marcus asked, now feeling like the teacher.

Scrutinizing the picture, Jason was lost for what he was supposed to see.

Marcus took his index finger and ran it down the road, covered with dust turned from pavement to a dirt road partially covered with broken stone pieces running off the picture.

"It's the road, located in an almost isolated area. Almost useless. Here you can see if you look hard enough. It turns to rocks covered with dirt, earth, or dust. Where does it go to?" Marcus asked.

Before Jason could answer, Marcus produced another Google Earth image. This one Jason recognized almost immediately and almost jumped out of his seat when Marcus handed it to him.

"This is it. I can't believe you found it." Jason exclaimed.

The Google Earth image was a replica of the map located in the envelope found in the chest drawn by Robert Hillman one hundred and fifty years ago. Clear as day, an aerial photograph of the road, a lake, several decrepit dwellings, the main house, and more dead vegetation. Encircling the picture was a tree-line surrounding what was formally known as Walnford Plantation. The picture looked as if time had started eating away at the buildings, farms, and roads with mother nature reclaiming the earth.

"If this is correct, it's almost too good to be true. Everything has remained almost the same as one hundred and fifty years ago. The same structures, the features are all there, and this is a real-time photograph, there are no cars, no people, no businesses, just abandoned buildings sitting there empty." Jason said with a smile.

"I thought the same thing. But I have to show you one last item." Marcus said.

Marcus passed him three pages of an online book titled "Frontier Justice, Lynch Mobs and Hangings." Jason read the article Marcus gave him.

"Three men hanged after being convicted of raping and murdering Lynn Walnford and her daughter Mary A. Walnford. One of the accused admitted they were hired to help run the plantation when the Walnford men went off to fight the Union. The longer the Walnford men were away, the more liberties the men began to take. When it became apparent the Walnford men were not going to return, they raped and sliced the women's throats to ensure their silence.

60

Amazingly enough, this was not the most atrocious act these men committed. The criminal men took over one hundred and fifty slaves, who were now free to the basement of the Walnford home. In a giant mass execution, the hired men began opening fire with their rifles from the staircase on the helpless men, women, and children until they had run out of ammunition.

When authorities arrived at the house several days to a week later, the smell from the corpses coming from the basement was pungent, causing many the hard lawmen to throw up before removing the dead bodies of the former slaves and burning them outside on the lawn. Many of these men reported hearing sounds and hollering coming from a large cavern underneath the property. The former slaves had fled into the cavernous underground to seek shelter from the onslaught of bullets. The continued racism of the Southerners who found the massacre would not allow them to assist the slaves lost inside the large cavern beneath the Walnford house.

Attempts to coax those who escaped the gunfire out of the cavern proved fruitless, or more likely little effort was put into helping the lost former slaves. The men, women, and children lost under the Walnford Plantation were now interred for all eternity. As the Marshall on the scene was unprepared or perhaps worse unwilling to mount an expedition to help save the poor souls who fled below into the cavern system below the house.

The three men responsible for the slaughter were hung, with two reportedly urinating on themselves as the sentence was passed.

"The fate of the Walnford family. The poor women must have put out the trunk per Robert's instructions before their deaths." Jason said aloud with remorse but almost to himself under his breath as he put the paper down.

"Let me ask you, with everything we have learned today doing our research. Everything you just read about the Walnford Plantation and knowing the property remains basically intact. Where do you believe the most likely place is that Robert Hillman hid millions in gold treasure?" Marcus asked.

"I believe we have an excellent place to start looking. We just have to go shopping." Jason said, picking up the newspaper picture of the identified man in the hat standing next to the giant crack in the basement wall.

14 – Abrams

Abrams started the seven-hour plus drive at three in the morning and made good time managing to shave off close to forty minutes, clocking the total trip at about six hours and fifteen minutes. He arrived in Walnford County just after nine am, driving directly towards Advanced One Towing.

The Advanced One tow truck company was run out of a converted storage facility and warehouse. All of the vehicles were stored inside the warehouse rather than outside, which Abrams thought was peculiar. Upon walking into Advance One Towing, a man sat behind the counter introduced himself as Beau. This was the same person Abrams had spoken with the day before on the telephone. Beau was eating a bowl of cereal and watching television when Abrams walked in. Beau looked as if he hadn't been expecting any business at that moment.

"How can I help you today?" Beau said upon seeing Abrams and hiding the bowl of cereal under the counter.

"I called yesterday about the Grey Lexus with the Texas plates." Abrams said.

"Yes. How will you be paying to take the car out of storage today?" Beau asked.

"I won't be. I'm a private detective working on a missing person's case. The owners of the Lexus went missing a few weeks ago, and the family hired me to look into their disappearance. If the vehicle matches their car registration, I expect the family will be up tomorrow or the day after to pick the car up." Abrams said.

"Wow, a real-life mystery disappearance right here in my shop." Beau nodded, suddenly feeling more significant.

"Can I see the Lexus?" Abrams asked.

"Of course, you can. Follow me." Beau said, leading Abrams around the counter and through a back-office area to the storage area where about thirty cars had been towed and awaited their owners. The cars were in lines of six or seven. The first car in the sixth line of vehicles was the Lexus with the Texas plates.

Approaching the vehicle, Abrams observed the spider cracked windshield and the dents on the hood of the Lexus. Before Abrams could ask Beau about the damage, Beau cut him off.

"The car was damaged like that when I picked it up. Got the pictures on my cell phone to prove it too." Beau said defensively.

"Did you happen to notice this?" Abrams asked, pointing to the bloodstains mixed in with dirt particles on the windshield and hood.

"Yes, the sheriff pointed that out to me. He said he thought it was some kind of animal or deer, maybe a wolf the car might have hit." Beau said.

"Did you see any dead animal carcasses when you towed the car?" Abrams asked.

"Can't say I did no. But then again, can't say where the accident may have happened either." Beau said.

"May I take a look inside the vehicle?" Abrams asked.

"Sure. Go ahead, it's open, and the keys are inside." Beau replied.

"The keys are inside?" Abrams asked, astonished.

"Yea, when the Sheriff found the Lexus, the headlights were still on, and the car was still running when I got there." Beau said as Abrams looked inside the Lexus.

"Where was the car found again?" Abrams asked.

"About two to three miles just past Speedy's restaurant and general store. Kind of a near isolated place out that way." Beau said.

Abrams opened the glove compartment and found the car registration, and the name matched Marc Harden. The registration vehicle identification number and the license plate were identical to the information Brooke Mueller gave to Abrams when he was first hired.

Abrams surveyed the car. No blood and no signs of a struggle on the inside. The interior of the vehicle was kept relatively clean. A woman's purse was present in the front seat. Abrams took the bag and opened the wallet located inside. He pulled the driver's license out and read the name Stacey Harden. Does a woman go anywhere without her purse? Abrams asked himself.

Abrams replaced the wallet in the purse but pocketed Stacey Harden's driver's license into the side pocket of his sports jacket without Beau seeing him do so. Abrams then reached under the steering wheel column clicking the latch to open the truck area. Abrams closed the car door and began looking into the truck seeing two suitcases.

Abrams opened the first suitcase. The suitcase belonged to a man and contained a shaving and toiletry kit, underwear, and several pairs of clothes. He closed the first suitcase and zipped the suitcase back up, replacing it as he had found it in the trunk before opening the second suitcase. The second suitcase contained a make-up bag, women's undergarments, and several changes of clothing.

Resealing the second suitcase and replacing the luggage as he did before with the first suitcase in the trunk, Abrams shut the trunk hatch. Abrams then took three steps back from the car. He didn't want to be rushed but felt he was missing something important. Realizing he might not get another chance to look at the Lexus. Abrams looked around the storage facility at the rows of vehicles parked in the lot.

"A tow truck company that stores its vehicles inside a warehouse instead of outside. A little unusual, huh?" Abrams asked Beau without trying to sound accusatory.

"Nah. Being inside helps keep people from trying to hop fences and reclaim their cars without paying. My daddy left me this warehouse when he died. He used to sell storage containers for people to use for excess space. But the storage space business never really sold well. So, when he died, I just converted the space for my tow truck company. This whole operation Advanced One Towing is just a one-man operation." Beau said.

"Looks like you keep very busy?" Abrams said, looking at the cars parked in rows in the warehouse lot.

"I tip the Sheriff a thousand dollars at Christmas, and he calls me first for any accident or any towing jobs which I give him a kickback on. But don't tell the Sheriff I told you that. The Sheriff's up for re-election, and I'm sure he would not want that getting around." Beau said, laughing.

"I don't see a lot of damage to these other vehicles. Is there something wrong with them? Am I missing something?" Abrams said, walking back towards the entrance with Beau.

"Yea, most of these cars, their owners just abandon them." Beau said.

"Abandoned them? Is that right?" Abrams said.

"Law says, I need to wait three years and take an article out in the paper or internet before I can take ownership and sell them. Happens a couple of time of a year anyways. Gives me an additional source of income after storing them for that long anyway." Beau said.

"The owner's families never come back and claim cars?" Abrams asked.
"Sometimes they do. Other times I wait out the three years and take the car to the auction." Beau said.

"Interesting." Abrams said.

"I'll be back with the owner of the vehicle soon; will she need anything like paperwork to claim the Lexus?" Abrams asked.

"Just the two weeks of fees at twenty-five dollars a day plus the towing mileage, which was about another forty dollars." Beau said.

"Thanks, we'll be in touch." Abrams said before leaving.

After getting some quick directions from Beau, Abrams's next stop was the Sheriff's office. The Sheriff's office was located in the county municipal building. Upon entering the municipal building, Abrams found a patrolman sitting at the receptionist's desk answering telephone calls. Abrams asked the receptionist to speak with Sheriff Reilly. The patrolman asked what the visit was in reference to, and Abrams handed the receptionist patrolman a business card with his name Abrams and the title of private detective printed underneath.

After taking a seat and waiting about fifteen minutes in the lobby, Abrams was escorted to the office of Sherriff Reilly. Sheriff Reilly's desk was immaculate and clear of any debris or clutter. His wall was mounted with pictures of himself fishing while standing side by side with his larger catches. Sheriff Reilly stood up from behind his desk, shook hands, and greeted Abrams, asking Abrams to take a seat. Abrams couldn't help but notice the Sheriff was on the short end of the stick when it came to height.

"Well, Mr. Abrams, what can I help you with today?" Upon reseating himself behind his desk, Sheriff Reilly asked.

"I am on a missing person's case, and I like to let local law enforcement know I am operating in the area as a professional courtesy." Abrams said.

"Professional courtesy, huh? Who exactly is missing? No one from these parts, I would have heard about someone missing certainly." Sheriff Reilly said.

"A couple whose car was recently found at Advanced One Towing a Marc and Stacy Harden. Their family reported them missing more than a week ago when they failed to show up in Tennessee. I understand you were the one who found their car, Sheriff?" Abrams asked.

"Yes, the grey Lexus with the Texas license plates found out past Speedy's restaurant. I remember. It was an odd place to leave a car in the middle of nowhere with the lights on and the engine running." Sheriff Reilly said.

"You forgot the blood and cracked windshield." Abrams replied, looking for a reaction.

"I chalked the car being found out in the middle of nowhere up to hitting a wild animal, a deer or something, and the driver finding the car un-drivable in that condition walked to get some assistance. There were no signs of foul play, or am I missing something?" Sheriff Reilly answered, not liking being second-guessed about his investigative methods.

"Does that happen around here often? People just walk away and go missing?" Abrams asked.

"No, never. There have only been three missing persons in the last thirty years in the Walnford County area, and most of those were teenagers back in the late eighties and early nineties. The station received the call about the Lexus from Speedy, the owner of the nearby restaurant. I went out there because he reported seeing the headlights in the distance. I checked the report out and investigated immediately." Sheriff Reilly said.

"It was Speedy himself that called you?" Abrams asked inquisitively.

"You are quick, Mr. Abrams. Yes, it was Speedy himself who reported seeing the car that morning." Sheriff Reilly said, becoming irritated.

"Thank you, Sheriff. I see you are running for re-election; I don't want to take up any more of your time. I wish you the best of luck in your election." Abrams said and, getting up, shook hands with the Sheriff once more before walking towards the door.

"I wish I could help you more with your investigation Mr. Abrams. But if you need anything as a professional courtesy, please let me know, and you will have my office's full cooperation." Sheriff Reilly said, sitting back down.

"Oh, one last question." Abrams said, turning around before exiting.

"Do you get a lot of abandoned vehicles out this way?" Abrams asked.

"I wouldn't say a lot. Cars break down and get towed away. Broken-down cars happen to the best of us. But like I said, no missing persons." Sheriff Reilly said.

"Thank you again Sheriff." Abrams said and walked out to the patrolman at the receptionist booth and asked him, "Can you please give me directions to Speedy's restaurant."

Abrams arrived at Speedy's restaurant and general good store after narrowly missing the turnoff from Route 72 and having to drive a few miles on where a road was once, but now the road had become overgrown with dust, dirt, and dense reeds. The dirt road went on for several miles until he arrived at the restaurant. Pulling up to the front of the restaurant, Abrams noticed he was the only car present.

Abrams almost thought Speedy's restaurant was condemned as he parked. There were no signs of life around or advertising on the road, which indicated a restaurant or store was ahead. It was as if the restaurant was situated on Mars. He put his sports jacket on, stepping out of the vehicle, and looked at the large sign that read Speedy's Restaurant and General Store. The large sign had been repurposed from an old Pepsi sign. The blue on top and red underneath waves in the circle pattern was still visible from the Pepsi logo.

Abrams walked into the restaurant's front door and saw about three aisles of items for sale, mostly candy bars, packages of hygiene items, and other car knick-knacks. All of the items stocked on the shelves would not be expiring anytime soon, but perhaps a better word for the things was overpriced junk. The store's back wall was where the refrigerated items, soda, milk, and juice, were kept. The refrigerators were emitting a loud hum in the room.

To his right, by the door, was the cash register situated on top of a countertop. The countertop extended from the entrance to the opposite end of the building. Eight stools were placed along the counter and behind the counter was the cooking grill. Sitting on a chair reading a paper was an older dirty looking gentleman, small in stature, wearing a white baseball hat and a greasy white stained t-shirt. The kind of person you could mistake for homeless and would try to and avoid, Abrams thought.

"Are you lost, or are you trying to sell something?" The man behind the counter asked.

A howl emanated from behind the counter.

"Be quiet, Duke." The man scowled at the old large grey dog of questionable breeding. The large dog poked its head up from the middle of the counter where the countertop could be lifted, taking a look at the visiting Abrams before returning to its bed and putting its head down.

"Don't mind Duke, mister. He's not used to strangers." The man said, putting the paper down.

"Now again, are you lost or trying to sell something? Cause I ain't interested if you are selling anything. And if you are lost, just go back the way you came and hang a right on route seventy-two. The main town is about twenty minutes from here." Speedy said.

"I'm looking for a man called Speedy. I heard he owns this place. Would you be him?" Abrams asked.

"Depends on who is asking?" Speedy said cockily.

Abrams produced a business card, the same card he had given Sheriff Reilly earlier, and handed the card to Speedy. Speedy stared at the card for a few seconds, maybe trying to determine what a private detective what want with him.

"I'm Abrams. Are you Speedy?" Abrams asked.

"I am. Did some rich relative die and leave me some money or something?" Speedy said with a chuckle.

"No. No rich uncles. I'm here because of the car you reported about two weeks ago to Sheriff Reilly. The car was abandoned. Do you remember that?" Abrams asked.

"I don't talk for free. But I do talk to customers. I'll talk all day to a customer. So, if you care to sit down and order some food, I'll be more than happy to talk to you all day." Speedy said.

Abrams obliged and sat down at the counter on the closest stool to where Speedy was and, picking up a grease-covered menu, ordered a cup of coffee and an egg, cheese, and bacon sandwich on an English Muffin. Speedy put a fresh cup of coffee on the pot and started scrambling the eggs and bacon on the griddle next to the grill.

"Most people they come here, they order a cheeseburger. Today in the afternoon, you are ordering breakfast, my good sir." Speedy said.

"You get a lot of customers out here?" Abrams asked, already knowing the answer but wanting to see if Speedy would brag about business.

Speedy laughed. "Out here. Not a chance, and that's just the way I like it. The few customers I usually do get come from Kingsford Chemical out in Alcorn County. That's a few counties away. I guess they come out here to nap under a tree or dose off for a while. They get paid by the hour. Nice guys, really. But other than an occasional local, I'm lucky if I serve ten people a week. That's on a good week, and that's just the way I like it." Speedy said, pointing the spatula at Abrams.

"Can I ask you about the car that was found two weeks ago? Where exactly was the car found?" Abrams asked.

"If you step out onto the porch when you leave and look to your right, I saw the headlights. I would guess the car was about two or three miles from here. Kind of lucky in a way, I guess." Speedy said while he was stationed at the grill.

"What do you mean lucky?" Abrams asked.

"Well, the time was just after five am, and it was still dark out, but I had to put Duke out. When I put Duke out, I looked over and saw the headlights just standing still, pointing into the distance back toward the restaurant. Anytime later in the day, and I might not have seen the car at all." Speedy said, putting the eggs and bacon on top of the English Muffin, placing it on the counter for Abrams.

"So that was the only time you saw the car then? You never saw the people in the car?" Abrams asked, taking a bite of the sandwich.

"No, I never saw the people in the car. At five in the morning was the first time I saw the headlights on the car but not the first time I heard the car." Speedy said proudly of himself.

"What do you mean?" Abrams asked, now blowing on the coffee mug, trying to cool the coffee down.

"I heard the car drive past my place about quarter to one that night." Speedy said.

"How can you be sure?" Abrams asked.

"Well, my bedroom is close to the road, and that road makes a lot of noise when cars drive on it with all the dirt and stones and such. You can imagine there's not a lot of traffic out this way. When the car drove by that night, I heard it. Like I said about quarter to one." Speedy said.

Abrams took another bite of the sandwich and wiped his mouth with a napkin, processing what Speedy just told him.

"And you called the police, the Sheriff after you saw the headlights at five am?" Abrams asked.

"Yes, sir, I did. You see, cell phones, technology, GPS, that stuff don't work out here. We are situated too low in the valley between the mountains; all that stuff just doesn't work this far out here. I used the hardline there on the counter and called the police. I was a little surprised the people in that car didn't walk over here and knock on my door and ask for help, to be honest." Speedy said.

"Is it possible they walked in the other direction? What else is down that road?" Abrams asked.

"Nah, that's old Walnford Plantation one way in, one way out. Nice lake up that way for fishing, though. The lake connects to the river through some outlets in the mountains and forest. Seventy-two passes on closer to that lake, but you have to walk through some tough terrain and woods to get there. Local fishermen may know some back trails to get in and out. But nothing anyone could go to for help out that way. Besides, it's another seven or eight miles to there from here. No, if I had to guess that missing persons of yours probably walked right on past this place, right onto route seventy-two. Maybe hitched a ride with some looney or something." Speedy said.

"It's a possibility, definitely something to consider." Abrams said, finishing his sandwich.

Leaving Speedy's, Abrams stood on the porch and looked into the distance down the road towards Walnford Plantation. Abrams was surprised he found Speedy to be a somewhat likable fellow. He made a good impression, was very disarming, and was a good witness. The time was getting late in the day, and Abrams still

70

needed to book into a motel and call Brooke Mueller with all the updates from the day and see if she could come up and get the car. There was a lot to think about, a lot that didn't sit right with Abrams. Several questions were left to sort out. Sometimes the best thing to do was remove yourself for a while, and the answers or questions would come when least expected. So, with that, Abrams left and headed back toward the Tunica area to check into a motel.

15 - Jason Matthews

The shopping list Jason and Marcus put together was very detailed and specific, four flashlights, extra batteries, three shovels, two pickaxes, two high-definition metal detectors, an emergency vehicle car kit with a flare gun, gloves, a folding hand truck, and twenty feet of rope. Jason and Marcus had debated the pros and cons of renting a larger truck or using Marcus' car for their journey. Jason typically enjoyed driving an SUV, but if someone looked in their back seat and saw gold bars, even a police officer would question them about this. A rental truck was considered. A dolly could be purchased to wheel the gold into the truck, they thought. Tammy dissuaded them from the rental truck, persuading them to take Marcus's car instead and utilize the trunk space. Best to keep a lower profile driving around than relying on an unknown vehicle which could break down.

After deciding on which car to take, Jason helped Marcus place the tools into the trunk of Marcus' car. With her yoga pants on and her purse in hand, Tammy came over to Jason and kissed him on the cheek. "I'm off to the gym for one last workout." Tammy said before heading to her car.

"Have fun, sweetheart." Jason said.

After Tammy had departed, Jason and Marcus sat at the kitchen counter drinking beers and looking at maps. Trying to determine if they had forgotten or missed anything.

"Should we have a cover story if anyone asks why we are out there?" Marcus asked.

"We tell them the truth; we are writing a book on the history of Walnford Plantation. Let's face it, just the little bit of information we learned from the internet makes a story about writing a book very convincing. Of course, we leave the part about the gold out." Jason said.

"Of course." Marcus said.

The following day, they awoke at just after four am and piled into Marcus' car. The plan was for Marcus to drive the first three hours, stop and grab a bite to eat at a diner and then continue towards Walnford Plantation. The car ride was unusually silent. Tammy slept in the back while Marcus and Jason infrequently chatted in the front.

"What would you do with your share of the gold?" Jason asked.

"I'd probably pay off my condo, buy a new car, get out of debt. I would love to travel to Australia on a sabbatical and study the aborigines and their culture. A research paper would go a long way towards gaining tenure at the university. What about you and Tammy? Any thoughts?" Marcus said after hesitating.

"We haven't even discussed the possibility of finding any gold. Tammy keeps telling me to wait until we find the gold before making plans to spend money we don't have." Jason said.

"I hear that. Still, it's nice to dream about being able to just sail away on a boat and living on a beach with some beautiful native girl with big jugs serving you Mojitos and blow jobs all day." Marcus said with a smile.

"To blowjobs and Mojitos." Jason said with a chuckle.

After about three hours of driving, it was time to catch breakfast and a restroom break. They pulled into a diner to eat some breakfast. Tammy and Jason sat on one side of a booth, and Marcus sat across from them. As they were getting ready to order, two rough-looking men and a woman came into the diner and sat at the counter across from their booth. The two men and one woman stood out from the other patrons because they were going out of their way to stare directly at Jason and Marcus sitting in their booth.

Jason got the distinct feeling something was not quite right. The three people didn't have any conversation during their meal which consisted of only coffee. Tammy sitting next to Jason, became visibly anxious upon seeing them as well.

"Is everything alright?" Jason asked, leaning over to Tammy.

"Yes, my stomach is just a little unsettled, that's all." Tammy said.

When the bill came, Jason took the bill from the waitress and said. "My treat." Walking the bill to the register to pay as Tammy and Marcus remained in their booth.

While waiting in line to pay, the smaller man from the counter who had a cross tattoo with the word savior imprinted underneath on his right bicep and had finished drinking his coffee came up behind Jason

"Is that your wife? She's very beautiful. You are a lucky man." The man behind Jason said, whispering in his ear.

"Yes. Yes, she is." A little offended and a little uncomfortable but not wanting to make a scene, Jason said, half turning towards the man behind him.

"Make sure you keep her happy. A good woman can make or break you." The man behind Jason said. Perhaps realizing he had overstepped his bounds, the man stepped back.

Before Jason could process what he meant, the woman at the register said, "Pardon me, sir, are you ready to pay?"

Ignoring the man, Jason stepped forward and paid the tab and left a generous twenty-dollar tip for the waitress on his debit card.

"What did that man say to you?" Tammy asked Jason when he returned to the table.

"He said you were very beautiful and to make sure I keep you happy because a good woman could make or break me. What do you think that meant?" Jason said.

"I think it means we should leave." Tammy said.

When they got up to leave the diner, the two men and one lady seated at the counter drinking their coffee had already paid and left. Getting back to the car, Jason took the keys from Marcus and started the drive to Walnford Plantation.

"You shouldn't have done that. It was stupid." Melinda said to Dominic Cross. The diner had cameras. They might identify all of us later on, just from that one stupid conversation you had with him.

They were parked a mile down the road, waiting to see the car Tammy, Jason, and Marcus were driving in to continue following them. They didn't want to take the chance of being spotted from the diner and make them paranoid. Instead, they just wanted to stay far enough back to let Tammy's car lead them to the Walnford Plantation and the gold. Tammy had phoned Dominic the night before, and Dominic knew what car, license plate, and route they would be traveling on the following day at four am. Dominic, Scooter, and Melinda had sat up waiting in the car at a gas station at two-fifty, waiting for them to pass by before following them.

Now watching Tammy's car drive past them for the second time this morning, Dominic pulled out, staying four to five cars behind them continuing to follow them.

"I had to know." Dominic Cross said to almost no one as to why he went up to Jason in the diner.

"You had to know what?" Melinda said.

"I had to know he was afraid." Dominic said.

"Was he afraid?" Scooter asked.

"Most certainly, Tammy's husband is a man who plays by society's rules and expects others to play in the same sandbox. People like him are always afraid of upsetting someone or not being politically correct enough. That fear is something we will use to our advantage. He will get that gold for us or die trying, believing us to be honorable like him and let him live. It will be the end for him." Dominic said.

"You got all that from a two-second conversation." Melinda said.

"Indeed. A man with no reservations would have put me in my place or put his hands on me. He did not. Therefore, he was afraid. A man who is afraid can be victimized." Dominic said, lighting a cigarette and continuing to follow Tammy's car but not following too closely or making it too obvious.

Part Two: In the Middle

16 – Speedy

It was late at night. Speedy opened his eyes in the dark from sleeping and thought he heard something scratching the wood behind the walls. Was the noise coming from Duke? Speedy asked himself sleepily? As Speedy rolled over, he realized he could still hear Duke sleeping in the bed with him snoring. Speedy got up and turned the light on, and opened the door to the restaurant area.

Speedy kept the back part behind the counter area of the restaurant as a one-bedroom apartment. In the dark, looking over the grocery store, everything appeared to be in order. Nothing seemed damaged or misplaced. The noise, the scratching sound, had stopped. Speedy turned the light off and was ready to get back into bed. The dog was now awake from its sleep with the movement of its master raising his head.

As Speedy sat down to get back into bed, a strange feeling overcame him. Goddammit, he thought. Can't I just make it through one night? He walked over to the bathroom in the dark and pulled his pajama bottoms down, and stood at the toilet trying to take a leak. He swore every time he wanted to urinate, it became more and more challenging to do so.

Duke stood up on the bed from behind him and started to bark back towards the door leading out to the restaurant and store.

"God Dammit dog. Shut the hell up. I'm trying to take a piss, for Christ's sake." Speedy said, turning and looking at the dog. Taking his hand off his penis, he reached for the bar of soap at the sink and threw it at the dog to get him to shut up and stop barking.

Taking total concentration, Speedy returned to the job at hand, trying to urinate. Then all at once, the stream of liquid erupted from his penis. As he stood at the porcelain throne, he wondered if peeing like this always felt so relieving. After flushing the toilet, Speedy walked the five or six steps in the dark back to his bed and just laid under the covers when Duke stood up again and started barking at the floor.

"Get down, you dumb dog." Speedy said, throwing the dog off the bed and onto the floor.

"Now go and lay down." Speedy yelled.

The dog sulked off underneath the bed with his head down. As Speedy laid his head down to go back to sleep, he heard the scratching again. What was that noise? He thought. A mouse, a raccoon, another animal trapped in the wall?

Speedy sat up and placed his ear on the wall. The scratching became much louder, and the rhythm had picked up as he could hear several scratches now like an orchestra or symphony of noise was being conducted. The noise wasn't coming from the wall, he thought. It was under the wood floor. Damn animals, he thought.

"I'll show them." Speedy said as he got up in the dark and behind the recliner in his small apartment picked up his twelve-gauge shotgun. Speedy kept the shotgun racked and fully loaded at all times. Five rounds in the chamber and five more rounds located on the side of the barrel. As he was getting ready to leave his room to look outside under the restaurant, he heard a loud cracking sound. A breaking of wood coming from inside the general store. Behind him, Duke barked from underneath the bed.

"Go get'em Duke, go get'em boy." Speedy said as he opened the door from his apartment to the general store kitchen area. Instead of obeying his master, Duke cowered under the bed and refused to move.

"Well fuck you then, you big pussy. I'll get them myself." Speedy said to Duke as he stepped out in the kitchen. Standing in the dark behind the counter with the store and rows of shelves in front of him. Speedy shut the apartment door behind him and raised the shotgun to the pocket of his shoulder, waiting to see if there was any kind of movement in the store.

"You should know I am armed, and if this is some prank, you should leave now, before you get hurt." Speedy said aloud, taking some dip from an open pack on the counter and placing a wad into his mouth. Speedy slowly walked towards the counter and flipped open the countertop to walk towards the entranceway door was near where the lights on the wall were located.

In the corner of his eye, he saw something run past the shelves on his right-hand side. The shotgun was already racked, and Speedy fired a shot blindly in the dark, tearing up some car deodorizers.; and placing a hole in one row of shelves. Items fell from their racks onto the floor, causing a loud ruckus in the darkness of the store.

Forgetting the lights temporarily, Speedy kept the shotgun raised in his shoulder pocket, re-racked the shotgun, and discharged the spent round, placing a fresh round in the tube. Speedy slowly walked towards the aisle where he had glimpsed the person running around his store. His heart was thumping in his chest. Every step Speedy took seemed amplified in the dark with the creaking of the wood beams on the floor under his feet.

Speedy heard what sounded like scurrying or clawing coming from the back where the refrigerated goods were kept. Speedy started to walk in the direction of the sounds, holding the shotgun pointed ahead of him, looking for signs of movement. As he finished walking the aisle, he turned and pointed the shotgun at something cowering in the corner. Speedy could see an albino creature in the darkness, looking at him with dead white eyes but not really seeing him. Instead of using its eyes, the creature seemed to be listening for movement. Or even smelling for him as it raised its head in the air. Speedy fired the shotgun at the albino center mass as the creature started to move towards him.

The shotgun tore through the small creature, pushing the carcass to the back wall of the store. Sticky blood littered the floor in puddles and splattered the walls and goods. The smell of gun powder filled the aisle, and the shotgun's shell was ejected onto the floor. As Speedy re-racked the shotgun and was turning around, another creature appeared behind him. The albino figure closed the distance towards Speedy in the dark. Speedy no longer had the space to turn and point the shotgun at his adversary. It was now close-quarter combat. Speedy tried his best to keep the shotgun between himself and the creature, which, although shorter, the albino was more forceful and ferocious, swiping at Speedy with its claw-like hands.

The creature landed a claw strike on Speedy's abdomen, slicing through his shirt. Being cut across his stomach was painful, but Speedy kept the shotgun between himself and his adversary, backing up and trying to preserve enough distance between himself and the albino monster. Speedy used the butt of the shotgun to hit the creature under its jaw, allowing Speedy to take a step back. But not being able to watch behind him upon striking the monster, Speedy had taken a misstep back into a hole in the floor. The crater on the floor was how the creatures were using to gain entrance into the store area. Speedy was able to catch his balance before losing his step in the hole. Returning the shotgun to the pocket of his shoulder, Speedy raised the weapon up towards the oncoming enemy in front of him.

Firing the shotgun, he was sent floating face-first into the air as his feet below him came out from underneath him. The shotgun blast misfired and struck off the refrigerated glass. Shards of glass and rivers of liquids spilled out onto the floor. The milk and juice glass refrigerator doors were shattered, sending glass scattered across the floor into the puddles of blood from the carcass of the previous creature. Speedy lay on the floor with the wind knocked out of him. When he turned over onto his butt, a set of hands with claws grabbed hold of both his legs and began pulling him towards the crater in the floor.

"They are trying to pull me into that hole, he thought." Speedy turned onto his back and began kicking at the hands, clawing and scratching at his legs. Not giving up, Speedy kept kicking, not letting them grab a firm hold of him as he crawled on his stomach to try and retrieve the shotgun he had lost when he fell forward.

As Speedy reached for and retrieved the shotgun, the creature he had shot at and missed rose up in front of him. Speedy, lying on the floor, grabbed hold of the shotgun and pointed it directly at the head of the monster, and pulled the trigger. A click happened. Speedy remembered he had not re-racked the shotgun after the last discharge as nothing had fired. Being pulled into the crater on the floor and with an adversary almost on top of him, Speedy fumbled. Attempting to re-rack the shotgun in a hurried state, the simple task of pushing the slide back and forth while ejecting a spent shell failed. The creature in front of him jumped on top of his chest and took a bite from his face. The albino being standing on Speedy's chest continued tearing at its prey, bringing its face closer to the face of his victim. Eating and clawing while the creatures below were pulling Speedy into the hole in the floor. Having a firm grasp of his legs which had stopped struggling. The brutes took their live prey, who was gurgling blood on the floor, and slid the crying bloodied body of Speedy into the hole.

17 – Abrams

When Abrams left Speedy's restaurant and general store, he was tired and booked himself at a pricey hotel. After checking in, Abrams carried his one piece of luggage to the room, where he picked up his cell phone and called Brooke Mueller from his list of contacts. Brooke picked up on the second ring.

"Hello, Mr. Abrams. Do you have any news?" Brooke said on the other end of the phone.

Thinking of Brooke, Abrams became disheartened, knowing how this was already going to end with her hating him for telling her sister was dead or most likely dead. But that was a conversation for a later time.

"Yes. I wanted to let you know I found your sister and brother-in-law's car." Abrams said.

"You did? Where?" Brooke said with hope in her voice. "Just outside of Tunica, a place called Walnford County, it's in Mississippi. A tow truck warehouse called Advanced One Towing." Abrams said.

"Is there any sign of my sister or my brother-in-law?" Brooke asked.

"Not yet, but I am still working out here. I'm calling because the tow truck company is charging twenty-five dollars a day to house their Lexus. Do you want to come out here and pick it up?" Abrams asked.

"To Mississippi?" Brooke asked.

"Yes, I could pick you at the Tunica Municipal airport, or even the Memphis airport its only forty miles from here." Abrams said.

"Let me call you back and see if I can get a flight out for tomorrow." Brooke said.

"Okay, keep me posted." Abrams said as he hung up.

After hanging up, Abrams got into a scorching shower and sat under the hot water for what felt like a long time. He let the world slip away off his skin as the beads of water slipped off his body. When he finished the shower and dried off, he saw a text on his phone from Brooke Mueller. She would arrive tomorrow morning at the Tunica Municipal Airport at nine am. He texted her back that he would meet her there.

After finishing his text, he slipped under the sheets of the hotel bed completely naked. He was tempted to put the television on but thought some quiet time to relax might put things in perspective. Abrams was asleep five minutes later.

The alarm on Abrams's cell phone went off at six am. It allowed Abrams enough time to re-shower and shave, get some coffee and a bite to eat from the hotel's complimentary buffet before heading to the airport to pick up Brooke Mueller. At the airport, Abrams waited by the exit at the baggage claim for Brooke. Brooke saw Abrams before Abrams saw her. She looked a lot more relaxed, dressed in jeans and a button-down blue shirt with a brown vest. Her hair was tied up in a ponytail instead of the usual curls.

Once in the car and driving out the airport terminal, Abrams handed Brooke her sister's driver's license.

"I found this in your sister's purse. I have to ask, was there any reason whatsoever for Marc or your sister to visit Mississippi?" Abrams said.

"None that I can think of, no." Brooke said, holding her sister's driver's license in her hands.

"Then what I am about to tell you does not get repeated to anyone and stays between us, understood?" Abrams said.

Brooke nodded in compliance.

"I have several questions about this investigation. Something strange is going on, and I haven't been able to determine if it's a coincidence, stupidity, or something more nefarious." Abrams said.

"What do you mean?" Brooke said.

"For example, do you know what the term BOLO stands for?" Abrams asked her.

"No. BOLO?" She repeated.

"Right, BOLO is law enforcement speak for Be On the Look Out. The term can refer to subject's law enforcement may be interested in or runaways or even missing persons or vehicles. This is a national way for police officers to describe what they are looking for across several states or counties." Abrams said.

"The reason I am asking you about BOLO's is yesterday in the warehouse where your sister's car is being kept there were about thirty other cars just left there. No obvious damage, nothing apparently wrong with them. The guy at Advanced One Towing, Beau, basically said he gets to keep the cars if no one claims them after three years. He has a financial interest in making sure these cars are not found by their owners. The question for me is this nefarious, coincidence or just stupidity." Abrams asked.

"The next question I have is about the Sheriff. Beau admitted to me that Sheriff Reilly takes bribes. The Sheriff is running for re-election. The Sheriff tells me there are only three missing persons in the last thirty years in Walnford County. The Sheriff of a small county would know how many missing persons reports there are at any given time. I Googled the Sheriff of Walnford County last night. He's been the elected official for thirty-five years. But if the Sheriff's the one calling the tow truck out for all thirty of these cars left at Advance One Towing in just the last three years, how many more cars previously have had their owners just walk away in Walnford County over the last thirty years? Again, am I reaching? Is this stupidity, coincidence, or is there something more nefarious going on?" Abrams repeated.

"Lastly, and this is a big if. What if these cars are getting towed before the BOLO's are being issued. What if the Sheriff for some reason is not following up on the car or does not consider the person missing because they are not from his county." Abrams asked.

"What do you mean?" Brooke asked.

"You reported your sister missing to the police a few days after she actually went missing." Abrams said.

"Correct." Brooke replied.

"But the car was recovered by the Sheriff almost a week before a BOLO could possibly be put out. Meaning, is the Sheriff deliberately not putting your sister's recovered car and the BOLO report together? Is the Sheriff deliberately not putting other BOLO reports together with the other vehicles in that impound lot?" Abrams said.

"Is it coincidence, stupidity, or something more nefarious?" Brooke said.

"Exactly." Abrams said as they pulled into the Advanced One Towing parking lot.

At Advanced One Towing, Beau showed them to the vehicle, and it was the first time Brooke saw the damage to the windshield and the streaks of dried blood on the car's hood. After looking through the vehicle a second time, Brooke paid all the related towing and storage expenses, costing over seven hundred dollars.

"Is there any way you can have the windshield repaired and billed to us?" Abrams asked.

"Absolutely. Probably just take a couple of hours to get someone out here." Beau said.

"Would there be a cost to having the Lexus dropped off to us at the hotel?" Abrams asked.

"In light of your missing sister and brother-in-law, I would be happy to have it towed to your hotel free of charge." Beau said.

"That's so nice of you." Brooke said.

"I'll be sure to leave the car keys with the front desk when I drop it off." Beau said.

"I can see what you mean with all those vehicles just sitting there." Brooke said to Abrams when they were back in the car.

"While you were going through your sister's car, I took some pictures unbeknownst to our host Beau of the license plates of some of the vehicles in that warehouse. I am texting the pictures of the license plates to my partner Allan Butler; he'll get back with me soon as he can to determine whether these cars are also reported missing or if there are any BOLO's issued by law enforcement." Abrams said.

"What do we do now?" Brooke asked.

"When I was at Speedy's restaurant yesterday afternoon, he proposed a theory to me that your sister and her husband hit an animal and walked back to route seventy-two and were abducted by some deranged individual at that time." Abrams said.

"Is that possible?" Brooke asked with her hand on her chest.

"Unfortunately, yes, it is possible. However, as someone more famous than me once said, when you have eliminated the impossible, whatever remains no matter how improbable, must be the truth." Abrams said.

"What does that mean?" Brooke asked.

"It means that if a car is parked on the road, more than likely there are two ways to go, one way is back to route seventy-two the other is to the Old Walnford Plantation. I would like to see this plantation and rule it out. Are you up for a drive?" Abrams said, asking Brooke.

"Absolutely." Brooke said.

18 - Dominic Cross

Dominic Cross was careful to follow Tammy and her husband's car and stay back a reasonable distance. If they slowed down, he went slower. If they came to a stoplight, it was practical to keep at least two or three cars back from them. Losing sight of them would require speeding up. Cross thought it was best not to take any chances if Tammy's husband or the fat boy looked back and recognized them from the diner.

A little after the three hours into the drive from the diner, driving down route seventy-two, they observed the car they were following pull off onto an unmarked road. Not wanting to draw the attention of their intended targets and give them advance notice, they were being followed. Dominic kept driving down route seventy-two and made an illegal U-turn a mile or so down. Doubling back when their car was out of sight down the road, Cross started driving down the unkempt road.

"It's exactly like she said, desolate." Scooter said, looking out the front seat window at the reeds and dirt that filled the landscape on both sides. The lone building on the road appeared on their right. The building sat alone on the empty stone pathway with a giant sign out front, a repurposed old Pepsi sign which now read Speedy's Restaurant and General Store. Even the lone building looked eerily dilapidated as they drove past at a slow speed.

There was no rush to catch up to them. Eventually, they would run upon them, but it would be better to cut off any exits or vehicle pursuits if they were outside their vehicle. Cross knew from Tammy that this road was the only exit in or out of the plantation. It would be better if they could catch them out of the vehicle and avoid chasing them.

A few minutes after passing the restaurant, a lake appeared on their right side. Trees surrounding them in the distance cascading up to mountains. In front of them on the horizon, the outlines of several buildings appeared. The buildings were built more of stone and brick than wood, which probably explained why they had withstood the test of time. The buildings whose roofs were made of wood did not fair as well. The layout in front of them was three buildings, two smaller derelict buildings in front of a larger house in the rear. Next to the house in the back were the remnants of a former structure built of wood that was no longer standing and had crumbled a long time ago.

Parked in front of the larger building was the car they were chasing. Standing in front of the building outside of the vehicle were three people watching their car approach. The three individuals, two men and one woman stood still, watching them drive up like deer, watching a hunter take aim, not sure what to expect or know who was approaching. Dominic sped up the vehicle, not wanting to give up the element of surprise and perhaps give the two men an opportunity to recognize them from the diner and run. Better to close the gap quickly and not provide them with any chance of response.

So, Dominic sped up the car and slammed on the brakes at about fifteen feet from them. The car grounding to a halt created a dust pool in the air from the car's back wheels. Scooter got out and quickly pulled his gun on them. Dominic turned off the ignition and jumped out, shouting orders at the two men while holding a gun on them.

"Don't move. Don't fucking move. I mean it." Dominic yelled as he approached the men, his right hand at a high ready, pointing the handgun at them with Scooter standing some yards behind him, also taking aim if any of the men decided to act foolishly. Melinda was also now out of the vehicle holding a large knife.

The men in front of them froze. Not fully comprehending what was happening and decidedly at a disadvantage in both firepower and size and stature. Dominic could see Jason getting ready to speak, deciding what he should say. Before any words could come from his mouth, Dominic pistol-whipped him in the head, causing Jason, who was taller but lankier than Dominic, to drop to one knee and place his hands on his injured head.

"Make no mistake, fat boy, I am in charge." Dominic said, turning after striking Jason and pointing the pistol at Marcus.

Dominic then came up behind Marcus and did a quick pat search to ensure he wasn't armed. He returned to pointing the pistol at Jason as Dominic ordered Jason to get up. Still wobbly on his feet from the blow on the head, Jason complied, and Dominic quickly did a one-handed pat search around Jason's waist to make sure he wasn't armed.

When he was finished pat searching Jason, Dominic stepped back out in front of the two men lined up next to one another and the female when Jason spoke up, now recognizing the man as the same man from the diner earlier that morning.

"What do you want?" Jason asked.

"Why, I want you to go and get me my gold, of course." Dominic said.

Jason looked at Marcus, and Marcus returned Jason's look, neither knowing how the man in front of them could have learned about the gold. Then, Tammy, standing next to Marcus, stepped out of the makeshift line and walked in the car's direction, standing with Melinda and Scooter. The sides had now clearly formed, it was two against four, and the four held all the cards.

"Surprise. I guess the cat's out of the bag now. That's right, your own wife betrayed you. You can cry now if you want; It won't change anything. I still want that gold. There is gold here, correct?" Dominic said.

"There's no reason for anyone to get hurt. If the gold is here, we'll find it for you." Marcus said as Jason nodded his head.

"I decide who gets hurt. Make no mistake about that." Dominic said.

"Hey boss, there's a car coming up behind us." Scooter yelled at Dominic.

Dominic turned and looked in the distance down the one road entering the plantation. He could see what Scooter saw, dust being kicked up and the sun reflecting off the hood of a car. They were still a minute or two away and with the sun in their face.

"No more surprises. Who are they?" Dominic said, looking directly at Tammy.

"I don't know, honestly." Tammy said.
"If you are lying to me. I'll kill you and then them. Understand?" Dominic threatened, pointing to Jason and Marcus with the gun.

Turning his attention back to the two men in front of him, Dominic gave them an order, "Don't move, don't signal them, don't even think. The best thing you can do for your health and theirs is to not even think."

"Put your gun down, out of sight." Dominic yelled back to Scooter.

The car drove up, kicking dirt and dust into the air. The driver was being cautious. After seeing the six people standing in front of him not move, the driver put his car into park. An older man was driving, and a younger woman who was the passenger both got out of their vehicle.

"Hello. I was hoping you could help us." The man wearing a sports jacket greeted them.

"Of course, what can we assist you with?" Dominic yelled back at him and then removed his gun hidden behind him. Scooter pulled his gun back out as well, covering them both. The man in front of them was clearly taken by surprise, and looking back at the female who was with him, he realized he was in a losing situation to act. He placed his hands up, and the female who was with him did the same.

"Move over and stand with these other two." Dominic said.

The two complied, stepping side to side, forming a line with the tall and fat man. The man who exited the vehicle was older than the female, who was much younger and very attractive. Dominic came up behind them and did a quick one-handed pat search around their waists and under the man's sport jacket to check for weapons.

"What are you doing out here?" Dominic asked them when he was finished checking them.

"I'm Abrams, a private detective. We are looking for her missing sister. You wouldn't happen to know anything about that, would you?" Abrams said.

"I'm afraid not. But it appears you are now going on a little scavenging hunt with us. You are going to cooperate, or I'll blow your pretty little friend's head off. Understand?" Dominic said.

Abrams nodded in consent.

"Now, let's get me my gold." Dominic said to the four of them.

"We'll need at least our flashlights." Marcus said.

"Go get them, fat man, but don't do anything stupid." Dominic said.

"Melinda, make yourself useful. Make sure both of those cars don't go anywhere."

Jason hit the key fob to release the trunk, and as Marcus was getting the flashlights from the bag inside the trunk, he was being watched by Scooter. Melinda walked towards Marcus' car and began slicing all four tires. When she had finished slashing the tires on Abrams's rental vehicle and Marcus' car Melinda then cut the wires on the steering wheel columns of both vehicles.

"Where are we going?" Dominic asked.

"Inside the house." Marcus said.

"Then walk." Dominic said.

19 – Abrams

Abrams and Mueller had driven the dirt road up to the plantation, and despite the afternoon glare from the sun in their eyes, in the distance, they had seen two parked cars and six people standing outside of a derelict house made of brick. Abrams drove past two other smaller buildings when he saw the people and the more extensive structure and decided this must be the main house. The main house stood two stories high and was missing windows, made chiefly of brick, the roof was missing patches of wood which had fallen on the inside, and the porch looked ready to collapse if a swift enough wind blew on it.

The six people were standing in front of their cars and seemingly waited there as if they had no purpose but to just stand there awaiting their car's arrival. This should have been a signal to Abrams that something was amiss and wrong. But his internal gut feeling did not register this as an unusual event to be cautious about. In fact, six people standing outside on a nice sunny day having a conversation didn't trigger any kind of reaction regarding danger at all.

With no gut feelings to consider or be wary about, Abrams parked the car facing them and quickly stepped out of the vehicle, where things had taken a turn from the bad to the how much worse can this get feeling. The two men standing next to or with the two women had pulled guns on them. Abrams had an initial reaction to the guns being drawn on him but had to keep that initial reaction in check when he glanced behind him and had seen Brooke Mueller standing behind him.

For every action, there must be an equal and separate reaction. In this case, if Abrams reacted, no matter how quick he was or lucky he could get, Brooke standing behind him could end up with her being collateral damage. Nothing worse than getting your client killed inadvertently. Better to take his time and wait for a better opportunity to arise, he thought as he half-heartedly raised his hands in surrender.

It was after the half-hearted, one-handed pat-search things got weird based on the conversation he overheard. Abrams judged there were two groups. The kidnappers comprising of two men and two women with two male victims. The victims were completely opposite, a short, overweight male wearing glasses paired with a taller skinny unathletic male. He and Brooke apparently walked in the middle of something completely unrelated to the disappearance of Marc and Stacey Harden.

Further, based on the directions the lead kidnapper was issuing, they were looking for gold. Gold Abrams thought that can't be right. He almost believed he misheard the lead kidnapper speak. Abrams did not believe in treasure hunts or quests. He did believe in what he could see in front of him, danger.

After the short fat hostage went to the vehicle's trunk, pulled a bag four flashlights out. The kidnappers' leader ordered one of the females armed with a sizeable army-type knife to disable the vehicles. When the female went to work slicing the four tires and disabling their steering wheels on both cars. The taller hostage-taker was watching, the shorter man in the trunk looking for the flashlights. With the movement of a fat hostage rooting through a bag and the female hostage taker slicing tires, Abrams was able to lean in closer to Brooke using the distraction and whisper.

"When they tell us to move, no matter the direction, slowly get out to the front of the group, and when I signal, run as fast as you can straight. Don't stop, and don't look back." Abrams whispered.

Abrams was able to convey this message without his moving lips. Brooke slowly but unnoticeably nodded her head. It almost looked like she was trying to catch her breath. The kidnappers had missed this exchange of dialogue because the shorter hostage had taken a flashlight to the leader of the gunman and handed it to him, and then turned and gave one to the unarmed attractive female hostage-taker. As the shorter hostage handed her the flashlight, he said to her, "Judas."

"Blow me." She replied.

93

"Now, now kids, settle down." The leader of the hostage-takers said to everyone in the group.

The group leader stood about six feet tall, weighed about one hundred and ninety-five pounds, and was muscular. He had jet black hair and a goatee. Despite his features, most noticeably, Abrams observed the tattoos on his right arm. A templar cross with the word SAVIOR written in ink below. On the kidnapper's left arm, the word NOMAD was tattooed in ink along with a picture of the Grimm Reaper with his scythe riding a motorcycle.

For years as a state trooper, Abrams had run across several types of bikers. He quickly identified both the males as members of the motorcycle club, the Nomads. The Nomads were notorious throughout the southern part of America and involved in prostitution, murder, gun running, human trafficking, and drug smuggling. The taller, quieter man standing to the mouthier leader's right was also marked with prison tattoos.

If he was also a Nomad's motorcycle club member, he could be even more dangerous than the man giving directions. The taller hostage-taker stood about six-foot-six inches tall. Both arms were covered with tattoos, and attached to his belt was a steel-linked chain wrapped around a metallic T-Ball bat. The bat was about twenty-eight inches in length and was light enough that if it was swung a full force and impacted on an individual's face would seriously fuck up a person's dental work.

The short hostage now was back in their four-person line and had two flashlights in his hand and passed one to the taller hostage.

"It's in the house, in the basement." The taller hostage said, turning without being asked, and began moving towards the house with the short hostage behind him and Brooke moving faster to catch up with them and get in front of them. Abrams also followed but was lollygagging, trying to get some distance between himself and the other hostages. Looking behind him, Abrams saw things lining up far better than expected.

The gunmen were lined up behind him in single file. First was the man he decided was the leader, who was keeping his gun pointed level at Abrams back. Directly behind him was the bigger man who also had his gun leveled. The tall man's gun was pointing in the wrong direction, and instead of being trained on the hostages, was sighted at the smaller hostage-takers back. Behind the taller man were the two women accomplices. One-armed with a large knife and the other a flashlight. Abrams did not consider either of the two women to be a threat at this time.

Abrams did not like having someone or someone's having or pointing a gun at him. Not wanting to walk into a situation he could never have the upper hand in, or when dealing with individuals with a questionable character, Abrams always put on his sportscoat. The same sportscoat Abrams wore into Advanced One Towing and during his visit at Speedy's restaurant. Today he was wearing that sportscoat because he was going into an area, Walnford Plantation, and did not know what he could expect, but it was an area at least two people may have disappeared from so far.

The sportscoat Abrams wore concealed a quick draw sleeve gun holster and in the holster was a Ruger LCP six-shot pistol. It was illegal. The firearm extractor would get the Ruger into his hand in two seconds. Abrams was aware he had the element of surprise. The man with Grimm Reaper tattoo had conducted a sloppy pat search, searching around Abrams' waist, and pockets before considering Abrams unarmed.

It was a mistake. Abrams intended on making the kidnappers pay dearly for that mistake. The intangible was if Abrams missed when shooting or if there was an exchange of gunfire. There was the potential one of the hostages, particularly of Brooke getting shot and becoming collateral damage. It was terrible business getting your employer killed. It was even worse getting someone who you cared about killed. Abrams would have to decide whether risking the hostages being shot and killed as collateral damage outweighed the opportunity to get out of this situation by potentially killing one or both of the gunmen.

"The only opportunity you miss one hundred percent of the time are the opportunities you don't take." Abrams remembered reading somewhere. If there was an opportunity to get out of this scenario before he or Brooke got injured or killed. He would need to act. It was a mistake bringing Brooke here with him now. He should have left her at the hotel or in Texas. He would have to be accountable for bringing her along, but that would be later. Hopefully, she listened, could keep her head down, and run when he yelled, "Run."

When the other hostages were about ten feet in front of him, Abrams acted as if he was tripping forward and as he was tripping forward but remaining on his feet, the quick draw sleeve gun holster produced the Ruger LCP six-shot pistol. With the gun in hand, Abrams tried to aim center mass while attempting to regain his balance and dodging a potential shot by the man behind him. Abrams turned and quickly fired the Ruger twice. The kidnapper behind him was at first stunned about the questionable beginnings of a fall and, judging from the look on his face, was in a state of shock when Abrams produced the gun, took aim, and fired quickly two times.

As surprised as he was by the gun and subsequent fire, the first kidnapper reacted very quickly, throwing himself out of the way and onto the ground. The taller man behind him, seeing that something was going on and seeing his partner fall towards the left, threw himself to his right side on the ground. The two rounds Abrams had fired entered the third hostage-taker, the female dressed in black who was carrying the knife. Two bullets aimed center mass on two taller individuals about five to seven feet behind him had missed but hit the third woman kidnapper at about eleven to twelve yards away. One bullet entering the cheek of her face and the other in her throat.

The woman dropped to the ground like a sack of potatoes. The woman standing next to her, seeing everyone else jump to the ground, also fell to the ground. Abrams never saw the woman hit the ground. He was already up and running and yelling for everyone else to run. Abrams continued yelling run to the other male hostages who had momentarily stopped and turned to see the commotion behind them. Only Brooke kept running as he had instructed her, and Abrams saw her run up the porch, opening the large wooden door, and get inside.

Waking up from their partial daze and taking their cue from Abrams, the two other hostages seeing Abrams run towards them, gun in hand, put them into motion. They turned and started towards the door. Brooke was standing at the threshold of the door, holding the door open. The kidnappers regaining any sense of lost momentum, began firing at them from the ground. Without stopping or looking while continuing to run, Abrams pointed the Ruger and fired once at the lead kidnapper. The shot Abrams fired was enough to have the gunmen cease shooting at them for the moment. Causing Dominic Cross to curl into a ball as the bullet struck the dirt in front of him.

Gunfire fired from the other kidnapper struck the brick and the wood of the porch surrounding the three men running towards the door for their lives. Running up the porch, pieces of brick and mortar debris from the building crackled around them as bullets struck the surrounding frame and doorway. As Abrams entered the house, Brooke was able to shut the door behind them. Abrams threw himself on the door and then slid down to underneath where the doorknob would have been but no longer was. A sliver of light emanated the room through where the missing doorknob once was.

Taking a breath, Abrams looked at the Ruger in his right hand, checking the ammunition, three-rounds left. One round in the chamber and two in the clip. Abrams couldn't believe he missed shooting the lead kidnapper three times. He looked at the three people in front of him. Both men were sucking air, out of breath from the short run up the porch stairs. The fat man had his hands on his knees, trying to catch his breath.

"Do any of you have ideas?" Abrams said, referring to their current predicament or what their next move should be or the fact that two killers were about to come busting through the door and kill all of them.

"The basement. We can hide in the basement." The taller hostage said.

"We need to move quickly then." Abrams said as he got to his feet.

Abrams didn't like the prospects of hiding in a basement. There were no avenues of escape, no exits, and they could be sitting ducks depending on the basement's layout. Worse, they could be waited out. The attackers could keep them downstairs, starving or dehydrating them to death without even coming into the basement.

But those were situations and challenges presented by an ordinary basement. Following the two men into the basement and carefully traversing a rotting staircase, the men in front of them turned on their flashlights. Scanning the basement wall until they found what they were looking for, a giant seven-foot crack in the wall and floor.

"We need to hurry; they'll be on us soon." The taller man said.

"I'm not so sure I want to go in there." Abrams said, looking at the crack in the structure of the basement.

"I understand, but if nothing has changed, on the other side of this wall, it should open up to a cavern system. If we get lucky, we can lose them in there or maybe even find a way out. Unless you have a better idea." The taller man said.

"You go first." Abrams said.

With that, the man who would introduce himself as Jason Matthews went into the crack in the wall, followed by the shorter hostage and then Brooke. Saying a quick Hail Mary to himself, Abrams followed in the darkness.

20 - Dominic Cross

Cross laid on the ground during the gunfight reaching for the pistol he had dropped when he flung himself to the ground and out of the way of the older man in the sport's jacket's bullet. Cross picked up the gun and, finding it hard to open his eyes with the adrenaline and dirt in the air in front of him, fired the weapon erratically. When the dust finally settled in, Cross was able to get a better aim. He saw the man with the gun running up the porch.

The man turned around once more and fired at Cross with the bullet missing in front of him. Scooter started to fire from where he lay down, and Cross, seizing the moment open fire once again. Dominic and Scooter both missed their shots, and the man with the sports jacket was able to retreat inside the door, and it shut behind him.

"Are you okay? Are you hit?" Getting up off the ground and dusting himself off a bit, Cross yelled at Scooter.

"I'm good. I'm clean." Scooter said, also just getting up off the ground but still excited from the action.

"Guys, I don't think your friend is okay." Tammy said.

Tammy was kneeling over Melinda's body, checking for a pulse. Melinda's eyes remained open, staring directly up at the sky. Forgetting their adversaries in the house for the moment, Dominic took his right hand and closed Melinda's eyes before picking up the large knife Melinda had used to slice the tires and placed it on his hip through his belt.

"I'm going to kill them." Scooter said.

"Yes, and we'll make it very painful starting with that old fucker. But we need to focus and get the treasure first." Dominic said, trying to put things in perspective for Scooter. Gold first. Killing second.

The three of them got up are stared back at the brick house, at the porch, and at the doorway.

"Scooter, go an take a look around the back of the house and make sure they aren't making a run for it out the back door." Scooter nodded his head in assent and started off to the back of the house.

Dominic and Tammy stood silently next to one another, over the body of Melinda. Neither one spoke. Dominic was feeling guilty over the death of Melinda. He didn't really care for her, but Scooter did. Scooter was his friend, and it was almost certainly Dominic's fault she was dead. Dominic's inappropriately conducted pat search and failure to discover the gun allowed the old man to get the drop on them and got Melinda killed. His carelessness had almost gotten himself and Scooter killed.

It was undoubtedly his fault. Believing he had the situation in hand, he had become complacent. Even when the situation changed and two unknowns had entered the scenario, Dominic still thought he controlled everything. A mistake he would not repeat.

Scooter returned from canvassing the outside of the house. He ran up to Dominic and Tammy.

"Good news, there is no backdoor. All of the windows are bricked up or have boards on them. There is no getting out of there. They're stuck." Scooter said.

"That asshole has a gun. That old fucker could be waiting right behind the door, ready to pick us off one at a time. It's a chokepoint." Dominic said.

"How many rounds do you have left?" Dominic asked Scooter.

Both men took turns examining the magazines in their firearms and counting their remaining rounds.

"Ten." Scooter said.

"I have nine bullets remaining." Neither had any extra rounds or magazines. This was a job escorting two weaklings to some gold. There wasn't any thought to needing more rounds than a standard clip could hold.

"Alright, this is what we'll do. We go up the porch. If we see movement, we shoot, but we need to conserve ammunition, so make sure it's a clean shot. We push open that door and then stay concealed on either side of the door. We do this tactically in case he starts to shoot at us again. If there's no shooting, we go in slowly, each of us covering a side of the room. Tammy will wait down here outside just off the porch." Dominic said.

"Remember, only one of them is armed. We want hostages. If we can grab a hostage, we can threaten the rest of them to give up. If that doesn't work, we kill them all." Dominic said as they walked up to the house and the porch.

"What about the gold?" Scooter asked.

"That's the only thing which will delay us from killing them all and is buying them some time." Dominic said.

According to Dominic's plan, the pair approached the porch, guns at the high ready position, waiting to see if the door opened. But the door didn't move. Dominic and Scooter moved up the porch, taking each creaking step slowly. When they got to the large wooden doorway, the two men split off, each concealing themselves behind the brick on each side of the closed door. Using the wall for cover, Dominic pushed the door open using the barrel of the pistol. Following the pistol barrel, Cross did a sweep with the pistol sight. While keeping his body hidden behind the archway brick outside of the door. Not seeing any movement inside, the room appeared clear of any danger.

Stepping inside, Dominic entered first, with Scooter following behind. Their guns still raised, looking into the main living area of the house. The stairway leading upstairs was no longer present, and instead, all that remained was a broken pile of wooden boards and debris which had fallen down a long time ago, making entry to the second floor almost impossible.

The pair completed a room-by-room tactical sweep of the first floor, searching what was formally known as the dining room and the kitchen. Both rooms were empty, void of anything, including furniture or pictures. The floors were scattered with dust, cobwebs, and dirt as the men walked on creaking floor beams and broken floor panels. There was no indication where their prey had run to or where they were currently hiding.

Behind them was a sound, a creak on the floor. Dominic and Scooter turned, raising their guns back to the entryway, towards the door they had come through. Standing at the doorway was Tammy.

"I thought I told you to stay outside." Dominic said, trying to remain silent as he mouthed the words.

"You can't find them, can you?" Tammy said in a neutral-toned voice.

"We are still looking, so keep your voice down." Dominic said.

"You can't find them because they are not here. They went into the basement, you idiots." Tammy said.

"The basement?" Scooter said

"Yes. Jason went after the gold. Can't you both see this was all a ploy or set up to ensure they got the gold? They were obviously in contact with those other two who showed up late in case something like this happened." Tammy said.

"Weren't they asking about a missing sister?" Scooter interjected.

"They are in the basement, the gold is in the basement, is there really anything else left to say?" Tammy said.

Opening the door to the basement. Dominic Cross turned the flashlight on at the top of the staircase. The wood of the stairs appeared rotted and ready to fall apart. Despite the creaks, the boards seemed sturdy enough to hold him going down as he took each step. As he traversed the staircase, he shined the light onto various places in the basement, looking for his quarry of which there were no signs.

When the three of them were on the basement floor, Cross shined his light firmly in Tammy's face

"Well, where are they?" Cross asked her.

Tammy turned to her right and, with her flashlight, illuminated a giant crack in the wall.

"The crack in the wall leads to a system of underground caverns. The system of tunnels is supposed to be about twenty or twenty-five feet down. That's where your gold is. That is where they went." Tammy said.

"Well then, after you, darling." Dominic said.

"You have the gun; you should go first." Tammy replied.

"Yes, I do have the gun." Cross said and pointed the gun at Tammy's head.

"An excellent point to be sure, now then ladies first, and don't make me tell you again." Cross pushed the barrel to the temple on Tammy's head, threatening her.

Tammy pointed her flashlight into the crevice in the wall and walked into the underground tunnel leading to the cavern below with no options or arguments left to be said.

21 - Jason Matthews

The four progressed from the seam in the wall down into the subterranean level via a tunnel. The only one who experienced any difficulty standing upright during the descent was Jason Matthews, followed by Marcus Robertson, Brooke Mueller, and Abrams. It was a steep downslope in the tunnel heading down, and Jason standing at about six feet one had to walk a little lower to avoid hitting his head on the tunnel ceiling.

The uncomfortableness of crouching down Jason was experiencing changed as the tunnel ended and led to a giant open cavern under the house. Reaching the bottom of the tunnel and peering into the extended pitch-black cave seemed endless. Even using the flashlights and scanning the cavern's darkness in front of them, the light beams from the light would not reach a back wall. Formations of large rocks that sporadically injected themselves along the floor of the cavern. Knowing which way to go in the underground labyrinth was going to be problematic. The man with the sports coat reached into his pocket and produced a cell phone, and although there was no cellular service, he was able to turn his flashlight application on his phone, which created some measure of light, giving the group a third working flashlight.

As they started to move, Marcus turned towards the female and introduced himself to the pair.

"I'm Marcus, and this is Jason. Thank you for saving us back there." Marcus said to the two of them.

"I'm Abrams, and this is Brooke." Abrams said, shaking hands with Marcus and then turning his hand towards Jason.

"What did we get ourselves involved with here?" Brooke asked.

"Apparently, my wife has hired the sickos upstairs to kill me." Jason said while his attention was still focused on studying the cavern.

As Jason started wandering off to explore the cavern, the man with the sports coat, Abrams, asked him, "Why would she do that? Try and have you killed?"

"Oh, I can think of a half a million reasons, give or take." Jason said.

"Nothing to do with gold?" Abrams said, recalling the conversation from when the man with the gun ordered them to get the gold. Neither Jason nor Marcus answered Abrams. Instead, the two men began surveying the cavern, carefully avoiding the rocks and potholes on the subterrane floor.

"We may be able to find a tunnel or pathway out if we split up and check the walls." As Jason said this, Marcus looked at droplets of water consistently dripping from the rocky ceiling above them. The many water drippings coming from the stalagmites above them created a light stream on the floor which flowed into a tunnel.

"The lake must extend under a portion of the house; we must be underneath the lake. If the water is dripping down from the lake through the earth and creating this light stream, it could lead to a way out." said Marcus said as he followed the shallow flowing pool of water. The falling water was creating a light stream or shallow waterbed in the cavern.

Jason could see Marcus and Abrams flashlights in the distance from where he was on the other side of the cavern. Jason found a wall and, walking around the cavern, used his hand to guide him along the border of the cave wall, discovered a tunnel.

"There's a tunnel over here." Jason exclaimed.

Abrams and Brooke, who were in-between where Marcus and Jason were, started to walk forward and exam a cavern's wall in front of them.

"There's a tunnel over here as well." Abrams said, illuminating a small tunnel with his flashlight.

"The tunnel on this side has water flowing into it." Marcus said as he got to the wall on the opposite side of the cavern as he followed the water flow to a tunnel.

Abrams, Brooke, and Jason all attentively walked back to where Marcus stood with the slight ebb of water flowing into the tunnel, careful to avoid any potholes or rock formations on the ground.

"Three tunnels, which way should we go?" Brooke said.

"All of these tunnels are considerably smaller than the one we used to enter through the wall in the basement. It will be tough traveling through these smaller spaces, especially for us bigger guys. There's also no guarantee we'll pick the right tunnel to exit through or that these won't end up as more confined spaces or even just end. At that point, we could end up stuck. That is if there is even an exit." Abrams said.

Looking down the tunnels, Jason knew going down these tunnels would require squat walking, crouching, and possibly even fitting through some tight spaces. As he was thinking about the prospect of crawling on his belly this there was a noise. A clicking sound was coming from the tunnel nearest to them and next to Marcus.

"Quiet, I think I hear something." Marcus said, turning back around and shining his flashlight down into the tunnel where the ebb of water was flowing.

The others started to move around to the tunnel where the noise emanated from. Marcus, not seeing anything, turned back towards the group. As Marcus turned away from the tunnel, a small albino creature jumped up onto Marcus' chest, taking its two claw-like fingered hands and grabbing hold of Marcus's head. Marcus, frightened by the monster jumping on him, was staggering, trying to remain standing and dancing backward while this creature was trying to take hold of Marcus' head. As Marcus lost his footing and fell back onto the rocky cavern floor, the creature placed itself on top of Marcus. Having knocked its prey to the ground.

As Marcus landed, he turned and laid on his side, attempting to get away from the monster in the darkness. But the attacker from the dark was already positioned on top of him. The creature using its mouth, chomped down on the side of Marcus's head, removing a clump of hair and an ear.

Marcus screamed in agony. Brooke scream. The screaming seemed to have awoken Abrams, who was frozen in place next to Jason. Both men had remained frozen with terror, watching the creature attack Marcus Robertson as the attack had happened unexpectedly. Abrams shined his cell phone light at the creature, and with a face of blood and a clump of hair hanging from its mouth, the creature looked into the light directly at Abrams.

The creature's eyes were dead white and pale. The albino creature stood no larger than four and a half feet tall and continued chewing on the ear in its mouth as Marcus wiggled beneath it, trying to escape. Jason was bewildered by what he saw in front of himself when the creature with its vacant eyes appeared to look directly at him. Then crouching on its hind legs was getting ready to take a second bite from its intended victim laying on the ground.

Abrams, terrified in place, raised his gun level with the creature standing less than six feet from him and pulled the trigger aiming directly at the creature's head. Firing point blank, the bullet struck the creature's head in the center and came out the back of its head as brains decorated the back of the wall next to the third tunnel. Blood poured into the small water-like ravine generated from the lake above, streaming into the third tunnel.

"Help me get your friend up. Help me with your friend." Abrams said to Jason, retaking charge. Coming out of his own daze, Jason bent over and assisted Abrams in helping Marcus get back to his feet. Marcus was crying and holding the side of his face. Brooke picked up the flashlight Marcus had been holding and shined it clearly on the dead creature now laying on the rock bed.

"Well, we're not going down that tunnel." Abrams said.

As Abrams said those words, Jason placed his hands over Marcus' mouth to muffle any cries and sounds Marcus was making despite his whimpering and crying.

"Shush. Listen." Jason said quietly to the group.

Behind them, in the long tunnel leading from the wall to the cavern they were located in, they could hear voices getting close, and the beam of a flashlight was present, then suddenly turned off. They had taken too much time exploring and then dealing with the creature's attack. Tammy, his wife, and her associates were making their way down into the cavern. If they tried to break for any of the other tunnels in the cavern, they would be seen.

Crab or squat walking through those tunnels with an injured man slowing them down and they would be sitting ducks for any gunfire. Their choice was made up for them. Go down the water stream tunnel the beast had come from or take their chances being seen heading for another tunnel and be vulnerable targets if gunfire erupted.

Abrams, thinking, quickly grabbed Brooke's flashlight and turned it off. He then turned his cell phone flashlight off. Jason catching the drift turned his flashlight off as well. Then silently in the dark, not breathing, Jason felt a tug on his shirt. It was Abrams, pulling on his shirt, pulling him towards the tunnel past the dead creature. Behind him, Marcus was being helped into the tunnel by Brooke. Abrams followed behind them, pistol in hand.

22 - Tammy Matthews

After being held at gunpoint and threatened, Tammy begrudgingly began her descent through the wall and down the tunnel. She had her flashlight in hand, and Dominic Cross followed behind her with a gun in one hand and a flashlight in his other. Scooter, who followed behind Cross, had the most challenging time trying to navigate the tunnel. While Tammy stood a shade over five feet had no problems navigating the descending tunnel, Scooter, who was six feet six, had to crouch down the entire length of the tunnel during his descent, putting strain on his neck and back.

About halfway down the tunnel, sounds emanated from below. At first, it was talking, then crying or arguing with what sounded like a scuffle. Tammy stopped in place, trying to ascertain what exactly she was hearing. Are they turning on each other, she thought? Dominic behind her pushed her forward, wanting to close the gap between him and their prey as quickly as possible. Jostling Tammy, Dominic urged her on, then a gunshot echoed through the tunnel. The group was standing still in the tunnel above when the gunshot rang out. The sound of the spent round echoing in the confined space below. The gunshot was enough for even Dominic to pause and stop his movement.

"If they are not shooting at us. Are they shooting at each other?" Scooter whispered behind Dominic.

"I don't know. Tread carefully and be ready." Dominic said.

Tammy turned her flashlight off with a sense of extreme caution and slowly moved the rest of the way down to the bottom. Dominic being prudent about not wanting to make himself a target followed Tammy's lead and turned his flashlight off as well.

Tammy's hands were so sweaty she could barely hold on to the flashlight in her hands without the flashlight slipping out.

Tammy was surprised to see such a large cavern open up before her upon reaching the bottom of the tunnel. Although she couldn't tell how enormous the grotto was in the dark, she sensed it was a considerable size. It was just like the newspaper article said, she thought. Could it be possible there really was gold down here?

Her eyes adjusting to the darkness saw some rock formations before her, and she quickly ran to one of the large rocks and hid, gaining cover against any possible gunfire attacks emerged in their direction. Dominic was unsure if Tammy had seen something before her, followed what Tammy had done, and took cover beside her and a rock formation. Scooter followed the motions of Dominic in the dark and could hear Dominic's movements in front of him as Scooter nearly tripped over a smaller rock Tammy had hidden next to.

After Scooter pulled himself up from the ground and settled in behind the rocks with Dominic and Tammy. The trio waited with bated breath for something to happen in the dark. Movement, sounds, maybe even just a slight noise to gain a general sense of a direction. But there was nothing. Dominic turned his flashlight on. He moved the flashlight beam from a kneeling position hidden behind a rock from right to left and back again. His flashlight beam could not reach the back walls from where he was situated, but he didn't see anything. Peering over the rock, Tammy wondered, where had her husband gone?

"Where did they go?" As if reading her mind, Scooter asked. Tammy could hear the sound of Scooter removing the T-Ball bat from the chain on his hip and getting ready to go to war in the darkness.

"We should stick together. Do a sweep from left to right to see if we can find them or where they went." Dominic said.

Moving slowly, with Dominic taking the lead this time. The three of them moved with each other until they found the wall on the left. Dominic frequently stopped the group when he thought he heard noise or movement and then continued on again. Repeating this process of stopping and listening several times.

An overabundance of caution on the part of Dominic, Tammy thought to herself. Something to consider, she thought. After a few minutes of searching, they came upon the first tunnel, the same tunnel unbeknownst to them that Jason Matthews had found just minutes earlier.

"They could have gone down there." Scooter said, peering down into the tunnel.

"Yes, they could have, but the room is so large. I want to know for sure which way they went. I want to know what they were shooting at." Dominic said, letting out a large sigh.

"We are losing time. They are getting away from us." Tammy said.

"True. We need to hurry this up." Dominic replied.

With that, Dominic started the group around the rest of the cavern wall, where they saw the second tunnel. The one in the middle of the wall, the tunnel Abrams and Brooke had stood over earlier. It looked exactly like the first tunnel, almost the same size and nearly indistinguishable from the first tunnel. Except this tunnel was situated across from the tunnel where they entered. Again, shining their flashlights into the tunnel, nothing appeared to be in there.

"We should finish up looking at this room before deciding which tunnel to take." Dominic said.

Upon finding the third tunnel, there was a noticeable discrepancy from the other two tunnels. Laying in front of the tunnel was the body of an albino figure. The creature lay on its back, bleeding out as its brains were scattered onto the wall behind it. The creature's blood drained into the water leading into the tunnel.

"What the hell is that?" Scooter asked.

"Oh, dear Lord." Tammy said, throwing up in her mouth just a little bit and gagging.

Almost unphased by the unexpected body and what the body was, Dominic Cross approached the dead creature and kicked it to make sure it was, in fact, dead.

"Well, ladies and gentlemen, with that, we now know what they shot at and, more importantly, which tunnel they went down." Dominic said.

"You can't tell for sure they went that way just because there is a body lying in front of the tunnel." Tammy said.

"Call it a best guess." Dominic said.

"No. I'm not going anywhere. I can wait right here." Tammy said, placing her hands behind her back, not wanting to appear to be a threat.

Before there were any objections from Dominic and Scooter, there was a heavy breathing and scratching movement that could be heard behind them in the direction of the other two tunnels. Dominic and Tammy shined their flashlights in the direction of the noise.

Sitting on two rocks with pale dead eyes staring sat an albino creature staring into their flashlight beams. As the group froze with the creature's appearance, a second creature appeared, settling next to the one staring at them. Both albino figures sat almost identical to one another small, thin, hairless, muscular, naked, blackened, dirty, big eyes, claw-like fingers, and crouching in a hind-like position, the same as the dead creature laid at their feet now. The difference this time was both these creatures had breasts and appeared to be female. The creature's rib cages became visible through their skin when they breathed. Both of these beings in front of them could not have weighed more than ninety pounds each.

Silence and fear met with surprise as fright ran from the pit of Tammy's stomach, through her chest, and up her arms. Perhaps seeing, smelling, or sensing Tammy tense up, the two creatures jumped down from the rocks upon which they were seated and sprung forward in her direction. They moved with surprising quickness and speed. Both creatures were closing the gap between them and Tammy in less than seconds.

Tammy, filled with fear, holding her flashlight in her hand, was frozen in place. But to her surprise, both Dominic and Scooter edged their way in front of Tammy. As the first creature attempted to jump up on Scooter, he one-handed slugged it under its chin with the metallic T-Ball bat wrapped in a steel chain. The beast landed to Scooter's left. Pieces of the creature's stained yellow teeth fell from its mouth across the rock bed. But the beast was able to continue to get up, ignoring the pain and stagger towards Scooter. Once again, Scooter connected with the T-Ball bat across the side of the creature's temple of its head. The beast being weak, from the blows, fell in front of Scooter, where he was able to smash its head with the bat as pieces of brain matter, blood, and skull exploded from the creature's head. The dead creature's body lay uncontrollably twitching on the floor.

The second creature who attacked Dominic fared no better. But the albino beast did go down more quickly and loudly. As the second creature approached Dominic, he raised his gun and fired

112

two shots, striking the creature's jaw and striking its chest. Both gunshots flashed like white in the dark. Tammy could see the hole plugged into the creature's chest and pass out its back when the second shot hit.

Dominic then took his knife out of his waistband and stabbed the creature he shot through the eye. Removing the knife, Dominic wiped the blood-soaked blade on the skin of the dead albino to remove the blood before putting it back in his waistband.

"Are you sure you would rather wait here instead of coming with us down the tunnel?" Dominic said to Tammy, asking in jest.

There was no response necessary. Tammy again acquiesced. This time, Dominic led the way forward down the tunnel with the small puddle-like ravine running through it.

23 - Jason Matthews

With the flashlight shining in front of him, Jason Matthews led the way through the tunnel squat walking while the others behind him did various crouch forms to move as quickly as possible through the tunnel. At multiple times Jason needed to revert to crawling on all four limbs like a dog while juggling his Mag-lite flashlight from hand to hand. This went on for the better part of twenty minutes, and it felt like he wasn't making much progress in terms of distance.

He felt dirty, sweaty, and tired all at once. His legs were exhausted, and just when he felt like he couldn't go on, there was a voice behind him.

"Wait for a second. Hold up." Brooke said as she was assisting a bleeding Marcus to navigate the tunnel while guiding him forward. Marcus' ear was eaten off the side of his head, and blood poured through Marcus' hands down his shirt.

Needing no further encouragement to take a break, Jason stopped and put his back up against the wall. He placed his head between his knees as he sat on his butt, trying to take a breather. The flashlight was pointed forward, looking for any more of the albino hairless creatures. But there was none. Not at this moment.

Brooke was now off to the side of Marcus Robertson, taking her brown vest off, leaving only her black long-sleeved shirt. She took the brown vest and placed it into the light flowing stream of water through which they crawled. Having soaked the vest thoroughly, she put the vest on the side of Marcus' face, which was bleeding.

"Take the vest and apply pressure to the side of your face where you are hurt." Brooke said to Marcus.

Jason turned his head away from looking at the injury to his friend and grimaced when he saw blood. When Marcus moved his hand to take the vest from Brooke, Jason saw where the missing appendage now no longer existed. Blood was still flowing from the scratches where the creature had grabbed Marcus by the head. The outer part of the ear was gone, with a clear set of jagged teeth marks on with what remained the inner ear.

"Keep the pressure there on the side of your face. If you need more water, soak it and replace it." Brooke said, applying the vest to Marcus' face, who squirmed in temporary pain at the applied pressure to the side of his face. Although he still had tears in his eyes and his glasses were gone, Marcus had stopped crying except for an occasional whimper of pain. Jason wasn't sure he could handle that pain level and tolerate it the same way Marcus had.

"We should really keep moving." Abrams said from behind them.

Jason cupped his hand, placing it into the water, and took a couple of sips to relinquish his thirst. The others seeing Jason do this with his hands took the opportunity to do the same. Not knowing when their next chance for nourishment might come. When he had drunk his couple of sips, he started back down the small enclosed tunnel.

The sounds of two-gun shots echoed down their tunnel from behind them. The four of them were limping along at a slow pace and had stopped and stared back with only Abrams keeping them on track.

"Let's go. Let's move. Now." Abrams said, and the slow crouch walk picked up to a brisker pace. The burning in Jason's legs frequently became too much, and Jason would revert to a modified crawl to let his legs rest. When Jason would resume his crouch walk to pick up the pace, he would maintain his balance by holding onto the wall or using his shoulder on the wall for support. After what felt like an eternity of crouch walking down the tunnel, Jason dropped to all four limbs and started crawling forward again. Although it had only been a few hours, these moves through the tunnel felt like an eternity wearing the muscles of his body out.

Unable to control his movements due to the exhaustion he felt and being so tired from walking in an uncomfortable position for so long, Jason's crawling became sloppy through the water stream, creating splashing sounds. Then there was a sharp change in the environment. Not the physical, but in the sensory environment of the tunnel. The air in the tunnel became fetid. There was a lack of ventilation, and a stagnate smell overtook the travelers.

"It's as if someone had broken the worst kind of wind?" Jason thought but was too polite to mention it at first. Still, he increasingly became sure the people behind could smell what was ahead of them. Then the group members behind him started to groan from the increasing noxious smell as they sifted through the tunnel. Multiple times members of their group would need to stop while they threw up or dry heaving due to the obnoxious odor.

Following the fetid odor, there then was the physical change. The ground below Jason became moister and darker. Then the scent became almost unbearable to the point Jason wanted to pass out. Jason crawling on all fours started to throw up. When he finished throwing up, he lifted his right hand and placed the flashlight upon it. It was then he was able to confirm the worse. They were now crawling through a tunnel of feces. Pure unadulterated shit left by the creature's; they were traveling through the creature's commode tunnel. It was as if they had been dropped and told to crawl into the sewer system.

"Why are you stopping? What's the holdup?" Behind him, Abrams asked.

"It's shit. It's everywhere. Mountains of shit, and we are crawling through it." Jason said, gagging on his vomit, dry heaving for the second time.

Brooke seeing Jason's reaction to the feces they were now crawling through, did vomit a second time. Marcus, much to his credit, was there to hold Brooke up this time. To avoid smelling the feces, Marcus wrapped the wet vest Brooke had given him with his left hand around his nose and mouth, holding it in place with his elbow while continuing to apply pressure to the side of his face.

Abrams passed Brooke and Marcus in the tunnel and picking Jason up by his armpit off his knees and back into a crouch walk position.

"Let's go. We are wasting time." Abrams said, pushing Jason. Jason needing that extra push, resumed his crouch walk forward. His legs were burning with exhaustion, and the lack of air further burning the muscles in his legs. Jason's clothes were stuck to his body from the sweat, and the feces smeared into all the exposed parts of his skin, hair, and clothing.

Finally, there was a sense of relief, but only for an instant. The tunnel in front of Jason expanded to an open smaller cavern. The cavern was about fifteen feet across in all directions. The ceiling to the cavern was almost twenty feet up, allowing a short reprieve from the crouching and crawling and the opportunity for Jason to stretch his long legs. Initially, his legs cramped, and he had some difficulty standing, but after walking in a circle on the mounds of shit for a few moments, the blood started flowing back into Jason's legs.

The floor of the cave was still made of feces. A chamber of shit, Jason thought as he leaned on the wall. Marcus exited the tunnel and stood up, no longer having to cringe his back but still holding the vest to his ear and nose with his elbow, and, upon standing up, he used his hands to tie the vest tightly around his head.

"The creatures have their own bathroom." Marcus said.

"Yea, and we are literally up shits creak now." Abrams said as he was the last to exit the tunnel and stand up to stretch his legs. The four of them taking a much-needed opportunity to shake off the soreness in their legs.

"Apparently, we don't get it. Intelligent species, monkeys, dogs, cats, they'll hide their poop or bury their poop or even fling it. These creatures have a dedicated tunnel to poop and pee in. They are organized, which means they communicate with one another and can learn." Marcus said to the group.

"You'll have to excuse him. Even in a life or death situation, Marcus is still an anthropologist at heart." Jason said.

Taking his flashlight around the round fifteen-foot cave, at the wall base across from the tunnel they came out of were two identical-looking tunnels. A left tunnel and a right tunnel. Neither tunnel looked very promising.

"I don't suppose anyone has a match?" Abrams asked.

Handing the flashlight to Jason, Marcus began digging into his jeans pocket with his right hand, producing a lighter, and passing the lighter to Abrams.

"You don't smoke. What are you doing with a lighter?" Jason asked Marcus.

"I bought cigars. Three of them, for you know afterward, to celebrate. That all seems so long ago now." Marcus said.

Abrams took the lighter, clicked the cylinder, and produced a flame. He placed the flame in front of the left tunnel and watched the flame dance back and forth, moved by the prospect of fresh air.

117

Repeating the sequence, Abrams again clicked the lighter cylinder and placed the flame in front of the right tunnel. Once again, the experiment repeated itself as the flame from the lighter danced, flowing back and forth from the air moving through the tunnel.

Abrams handed the lighter back to Marcus, who placed the lighter back into his pocket. Jason then handed Marcus back his flashlight.

"Wind carrying fresh air, coming from both directions. How far away or which tunnel to take is the question. But we should decide quickly." Abrams said.

"I have a plan." Jason said, stepping over to Abrams. Give me your cell phone flashlight. Abrams did as Jason asked and handed him his cell phone. Jason, in turn, handed Abrams his Maglite flashlight.

"You three take the tunnel on the right. I'll wait here, and when I see them, I'll lead them in the opposite direction down the left tunnel." Jason said when the handoff of flashlights was completed.

"That's absurd." Marcus said, holding the vest across his nose and up towards his bleeding ear.

"More to the point, it's suicide." Marcus reiterated.

"This entire thing is my fault, Marcus, my wife, my map, my buying those chests, my plan, my decision. You expressed your opinion about my wife coming along from the start, and I didn't listen to you." Jason said.

"We are better off staying together. We can fight these things together or your wife's friends together. But we have a better chance together, as a team." Abrams said.

"It's time to stop lying to yourselves. We can't fight what's in front of us if we are worried about what is trying to kill us from behind us. At least this way, you'll only have to worry about what you see in front of you. You'll have a chance. Now go." Jason said, pointing the cell phone light towards the right tunnel.

Abrams went first with the Mag-lite but, before resuming his crouched walk position, said to Jason, "That's my cell phone. It's expensive. I want it back. You will return that to me." With those words, Abrams disappeared down into the right tunnel.

"Don't do anything stupid. If you see them run." Marcus said, shaking Jason's hand before following Abrams and disappearing down the tunnel. Lastly, Brooke wished him luck and followed behind Marcus.

There was nothing for Jason to do but wait in the room of shit and stand there. He stretched his legs and shook them out, trying to keep them loose. He looked at the cell phone Abrams left him and switched the light off to see how much battery was left. Eight percent, the cellular bar in the right-hand corner was nearly drained. Familiar words appeared across the screen. Battery requires charging. Please recharge the battery. Wonderful, it won't be long now before the light from this cell phone burns out, Jason thought.

24 - Dominic Cross

After being attacked by those monstrosities, Dominic only had one thought on his mind. Revenge. It kept him going while he crouched through what felt like miles of tunnel. Revenge. The thought took hold of him, and he wouldn't let go. There was no way he was going to let those nerds and an old man beat him. Revenge played on in his mind. They killed Melinda and almost killed him and Scooter.

"Can we please take a break? My legs are killing me." Tammy said behind him, complaining.

"No. We are behind enough and losing ground every minute. We need to catch up." Dominic said.

"We are losing Scooter; he's falling way behind. A bigger guy just doesn't travel as fast in here." Tammy said.

It was the first thing Tammy said that made any sense, Dominic thought as he looked behind him and saw the glimmer of the flashlight which Tammy held previously but had given up to Scooter before entering this tunnel. His long legs and that he wasn't in the best shape put Scooter at a severe disadvantage in these tunnels.

"Alright, we'll wait here. Allow Scooter to catch up." Dominic said, positioning himself with the gun between his legs and the flashlight shining at the top of the tunnel, so both he and Tammy had some light. Tammy, drenched in sweat, came and sat next to Dominic, wiping her forehead with her sleeve.

"I think one of them is hurt." Dominic said.

"What makes you think that?" Tammy asked, cupping her hand the same way Jason, her husband, had earlier and taking a sip of the little ravine water.

Dominic took the flashlight and put the beam on the ground next to them. Drops of black formed a trail down the tunnel up ahead.

"Its blood. Couldn't be anything else." Dominic said.

"How do you think they got hurt?" Tammy asked.

"Probably during the creature attack. But it doesn't matter. The fact one of them is bleeding means they'll travel slower. For your sake, we need to catch up before they find a way out of here." Dominic said.

"Is that a threat?" Tammy asked, staring at him.

"Don't pretend to be all offended. You and I both know, if they get away, it's your ass they'll go after and talk to the police about." Dominic said.

"What about you?" Tammy said.

"You are the only one who knows who Scooter and I are. I can make you disappear at any time. Frankly, the only reason you are still alive and not back with Melinda on the ground is because if there is no gold, you better come up with some money real fast." Dominic said this statement as a matter of fact. His voice was not changing. He looked over, and Scooter was closing in on them.

"How are you doing there, buddy?" Dominic asked Scooter.

Looking as if he would collapse at any moment, Scooter gave him a thumbs-up as he sucked wind, trying to catch his breath. Beads of sweat ran down his face. While Dominic and Tammy had been crouching down and walking through the tunnels, Scooter had to get down on all four limbs and crawl through the tunnel making slow progress thanks to his size.

"You should take a break here. Catch up when you can." Dominic said. Scooter took the hint reading in-between the lines. He was slowing them down.

"I'll rest here, just for a few minutes, and then catch up. I'll be right behind you." Scooter said. Scooter was too tired to argue and began waving his hand to them to start moving.

"Fair enough. Let's go find your husband and his friends." Dominic said. Turning his gaze back to Tammy as they once again starting down the tunnel.

After the short break with Tammy, Dominic felt renewed with both purpose and energy. He was making good time crouching and walking through the tunnel. Scooter had let him down. Scooter had been shown up when Melinda was killed by some nobody, and Scooter's heart didn't seem interested in finding her killer. He was on his own, and quite frankly, it was the way Dominic preferred

121

things. Dominic was always a loner at heart. Having others with him meant he had to listen to their opinions and account for them. On his own, there were no rules other than the ones Cross made up as he went along.

About ten minutes after leaving Scooter behind, the air quality in the tunnel changed in terms of smell. The smell slowed Dominic down as his breathing in of the putrid air quality became hampered. It smelled like sewage, he thought. The sewage smell changed and actually got worse, now smelling like shit. He couldn't believe how bad it smelled.

Dominic looked behind him, and Tammy was now frequently stopping to gag when she took in big gasps of air. He decided he couldn't wait on Tammy either. She, too, was beginning to slow him down. Dominic started to outpace her. Then the texture of the ground became mushier as Dominic crouch walked across it until he accidentally dropped his flashlight in the mush, which covered the floor.

"Oh shit." Dominic said to himself as he stared at shit now covering the flashlight. Better not to drop the handgun, he thought.

Trekking through the tunnel with the air almost unbreathable, Dominic was now becoming winded and threw up once in his mouth, gagging on the vomit he swallowed. His throat began drying out from the retching of the throw-up he was consuming. He did not want to stay in one spot for too long, hoping this tunnel of shit would end soon. It reminded Dominic of his favorite movie, the Shawshank Redemption, where Tim Robbins crawls through the pipe of shit to his freedom. Comparing himself to Andy Dufrene in the Shawshank Redemption movie kept Dominic moving.

Now easily outdistancing both Tammy and Scooter, Dominic saw an end to the tunnel. The flashlight he struggled to carry illuminated a larger opening up ahead to a cave. Cross hoped the cave ahead would give him a break and allow him to stretch and get away and from the smell. Cross using his last bits of energy and second wind, hurried to rush towards that opening of the tunnel, looking for any bits of fresh air.

Not wanting to rush into one of those creatures, as Dominic reached the opening of the smaller cavern, he slowed down momentarily. He saw the floor was still littered with shit. The smaller cavern was nowhere near as large as the one they had come down out of the wall through. In fact, he could see ahead to the wall in front of him using the flashlight covered in shit. There were two tunnels ahead of him.

His legs burned as he was finishing his crouch walk, the light still shining ahead of him. No monsters, no movements, no adversaries, a chance to stand up and regain himself before pressing on, he thought. As he was exiting the tunnel still in the crouch, a black figure emerged from the wall. Dominic almost didn't see the figure in black movements at all. Being focused on the goal of standing up after trekking through endless yards of shit, he didn't take the time to focus the flashlight around the small cavern.

The figure in black waited until Dominic stuck his head out from the tunnel and lunged at him with a rock striking him in the head with a piece of stone. Dominic, whose legs were still wobbly from the trek through the tunnel, lost both the flashlight and the gun on the floor as he fell into the shit beneath him. Dominic reacted quickly to the blow to the head. Dazed but not out, Cross had taken plenty of hits to the head in past fights. Opening his eyes, Cross recovered from the attack and began scrambling for the gun through the mounds of shit on the floor. Placing his hands in the piles of feces on the floor, searching through the shit. Relying only on the sense of touch while looking for the lost handgun.

The figure in black who attacked Dominic failed to follow up right away on his advantage, having also fallen over in the attack with the piece of stone. Still, the figure shrouded in black already up on his feet and began kicking Dominic in the ribs. It wasn't a very sturdy kick, Dominic thought. As the figure in black tried to kick Dominic a second time, Dominic caught the figure's leg and took the attacker down to the ground. Cross had difficulty holding onto the portion of the figure's leg in black because his legs were so slimy. The attacker in black was covered from head to toe in brown feces and was starting to slip away. Dominic then realized who his attacker was; the figure covered in shit was Tammy's husband, Jason Matthews.

Putting his attacker into perspective gave Dominic a new zeal for the fight. This is a fight despite the number of advantages Jason would have; Dominic should win ninety-nine percent of the time. Reassured he was fighting Jason, Dominic resumed his attempt to grab Jason by the legs. Jason had covered himself in feces and used the darkness and feces as camouflage, and hid along the wall, waiting to attack the first person out of the tunnel.

Dominic now remembered the knife on his belt, still holding Jason's leg. Dominic reached for the knife in his belt. As he brought the blade out, Jason, who was now trying to kick his legs free from Dominic, stared. Dominic could see Jason's eyes in the darkness get bigger at seeing the knife. Even in the dark, Dominic could see Jason's eyes grow brighter with fear. Jason was aware of the coming knife attack began kicking at Dominic's face with his feet. One foot caught Dominic on the nose and was followed up with a kick that caught Dominic's throat.

Dominic, still holding the blade but unable to breathe due to the blow that landed on his throat, let go of Jason's legs, and Dominic began slashing violently at Jason's legs with the knife. The second swipe caught Jason's jeans, and Dominic saw blood. It was that third kick to Dominic which sent Dominic onto his back.

What seemed like good fortune for Jason, kicking Dominic onto his back, worked to Dominic's advantage immensely. As he fell to the ground, Dominic's left hand, the hand not holding the knife, felt something metallic. Dominic's instincts took over immediately, and he placed his left hand on the grip of the gun and sat up and pointed the gun at Jason, who was in the process of fleeing, ducking into the leftmost tunnel.

Cross got to his feet and ran over to the left tunnel entrance and, going into a kneeling position, fired three rounds after Jason. Not seeing anything, not hearing anything coming from the tunnel, Dominic went and retrieved the flashlight and shined the light into the tunnel. There were no tracks, no blood, and no Jason Matthews in the tunnel. The bullets he fired after Jason Matthews had missed. Then someone grabbed his right shoulder from behind. Dominic, startled from the touch coming up from behind him, fell down into the feces on the floor as his back hit the wall.

"What's going on? Are you ok? My God, Dominic, you are bleeding from your head?" Tammy Matthews said as she now stood over him, holding a flashlight.

Dominic taking a second to wipe the shit off his hand, put his hand up to his head and felt the blood trickle down from where Jason struck him with the rock.

"Your husband Jason just attacked me. He was covered in shit, camouflaged, and ambushed me when I came out of the tunnel." Dominic said.

"Where is he now? I heard gunshots; did you kill him?" Tammy asked.

"He fled down this tunnel. I fired after him, but I must have missed him. I have to admit your husband has bigger balls than I initially gave him credit for." Dominic said.

"I can't believe he actually stood up for himself. What now? Do we wait for Scooter to catch up?" Tammy said.

"Fuck no. We go after that prick." Dominic said, and being more careful, he and Tammy started into the left tunnel chasing after Jason.

25 - Tammy Matthews

In the two weeks preceding their excursion to Mississippi, Tammy Matthews planned to kill her husband. Tammy pieced the project together while taking a shower following the impromptu meeting in the hotel with Dominic Cross and his friends Scooter and Melinda. If she thought they would kill her husband for twenty thousand dollars, she would be underestimating their greed. The three of them were nothing short of parasites. But, in Tammy's mind, she was already ahead of them, thinking three or four moves ahead.

Eventually, the parasites would keep calling and bleed her dry, blackmail, threats, even extortion. She hadn't even been truthful with them. Her husband's life insurance was valued at over five hundred thousand dollars through the university, not one hundred thousand dollars. Tammy decided she would need to plan to exterminate all the witnesses and leave her completely innocent.

As fate would have it, when she returned home from the hotel meeting with Dominic, Jason had produced the idea for his own death. Meeting with her husband, Jason became frenzied talking about a treasure map and lost confederate gold. Tammy believed the concept of lost gold was ridiculous. But there was something there to appeal to Dominic Cross and his greed. The opportunity to travel to Mississippi from Georgia could work in her favor if she planned everything correctly.

It would require two pieces coming together, Dominic to buy in and Tammy's ability to get hold of a gun. As it turned out, both happened in short order. Dominic bought in quicker than she imagined, and the prospect of gold and greed blinded Cross from seeing clearly.

The second part of getting hold of a gun would be a little more challenging. The day Tammy called Dominic to discuss Mississippi and the gold, Tammy was calling from a firing the

Champion Firing Range. Tammy signed into the shooting range on a one-day pass using a driver's license she had stolen from a friend week prior. Tammy rented a gun using cash but decided against walking out with the pistol. There were cameras everywhere at the range. She did the next best thing in her mind. She positioned herself on the firing range next to a man she thought she could manipulate and asked for his help.

The man in the following firing range, Michael, seemed was friendly and was helpful. Tammy would exploit Michael's characteristics, his generosity, and his niceness and use them to her advantage and against him. Playing helpless, she had Michael teach her how to use a gun, load, reload and fire a weapon, about feet position, and most importantly, he said gun safety. Although Tammy believed the part about gun safety was just an opportunity for Michael to get close to her. While Michael trained Tammy, she asked him.

"I bet you have a lot of guns at home?" Tammy asked Michael when he was close to her.

"Yes, I do." Michael said

"How many guns do you have?" Tammy asked, flirting.

"Twenty-five or so, mostly pistols, some rifles, a couple of antiques, and a shotgun." Michael answered.

At the end of the training session, Michael had gathered enough nerve to ask Tammy out.

"If you are not busy, maybe we could get together for dinner sometime." Michael asked her.

"Why don't we go to your house now." Tammy said, being direct.

Tammy followed Michael in her car, and arriving at his house, Michael suddenly became very nervous, unsure what he should do or how to make the next move. His inexperience with women showed. So, Tammy took the lead.

"Why don't you take me for a tour of your house." Tammy said.

The tour was short as it was a three-bedroom, one-and-a-half-bath that needed a woman's touch in the worst possible way. At the end of the tour, the last room to be shown was the master bedroom. Tammy, again giving strong signals of interest, sat down on Michael's bed. When Michael made his move on Tammy,

Tammy reminded him who was in charge and asked Michael to take a shower first.

As Michael went to take a shower, Tammy used the time to go through Michael's bedroom. In the first spot, Tammy looked found what she was searching for a handgun. The pistol was hidden underneath the pillow. Men lacked any creative imagination, she thought.

When Michael emerged from the shower wearing a towel, Tammy lay on his bed, pistol in hand, wearing only her panties and bra.

"Look what I found under my pillow." Tammy said, pointing the gun at Michael.

"I leave it there in case of an intruder or burglar. Easy access." Michael said, moving carefully in the bedroom with the towel wrapped around his waist. Michael did not appreciate having his own gun pointed in his direction and thinking Tammy's behavior with the firearm was not very funny. At the same time, Michael did not want to upset the woman who lay essentially naked on his bed.

"Easy access, huh?" Tammy said, spreading her legs revealing her crotch to him.

"Yes, easy access." Michael said, his erection showing through the towel as he positioned himself on the bed next to Tammy.

"Would you mind if I borrowed this gun for the weekend, so I can practice. I promise I will bring it back the next time I see you." Tammy said as he began to kiss on Michael's neck.

She could have asked Michael for a million dollars; the answer would have been yes. He was going to get sex and would not want to ruin the mood by telling her no.

"Of course, no problem." Michael said, unwrapping his towel and getting into the bed with Tammy.

The sex was plain, ordinary, boring, and unimaginative. It was the complete opposite of the great sex Tammy had been experiencing the last few months seeing Dominic Cross where every encounter was titillating. The only pleasure from the experience was knowing Michael just handed her the weapon to rid herself of Dominic Cross and his friends.

The plan Tammy set in motion was simple yet elegant. The police would find her story wholly reliable and could fact-check all they wanted. Tammy, Jason, and Marcus would go away on a vacation trip to Mississippi. A vacation they were taking to research a book her History professor husband and his friend were writing. The three of them were accosted by these killers, all of which had prior records for murder or other crimes. They were gang members and ex-felons. After they killed her husband and his friend, they were going to kill and rape Tammy. Luckily, Tammy had a gun a friend lent her for the vacation, and she was able to defend herself from the assault and kill these murderers in the process.

The police could verify everything. The fact the gun was lent to her by Michael could be quickly be confirmed by the police. The men who attacked and killed her husband and his friend had criminal records. Lastly, there would be no witnesses to testify Tammy's version was incorrect. She would play the crying wife, victim to the tune of five hundred thousand dollars.

With her plan put into motion arriving at Walnford Plantation, Dominic, Scooter, and Melinda had taken control and put Jason and Marcus at a disadvantage from the start of the encounter. Tammy wished Dominic would shoot and kill them right there, but Dominic wanted the gold. How long would it take for Dominic to put bullets into both Jason and Marcus after seeing there was no gold, she wondered? In any case, Tammy had the gun Michael gave her stashed away behind her back, under her shirt, hidden from sight.

Then the wild card emerged, a man in a sports jacket and a younger woman. The plantation was supposed to be isolated. Dominic quickly took control of them as well, but for some reason, he kept them alive. With all four people in custody at gunpoint, Tammy once again felt in control. However, the feeling was fleeting as the man in the sportscoat started a shootout. Extra bullets would be hard to explain to the police, but not impossible, Tammy thought, leaving any survivors other than herself would be harder to explain. She thought of the gun behind her back. Should she use it?

Pulling a gun out would produce unintended consequences of having Dominic Cross and Scooter both asking questions about the trust she had in them and why she needed to carry a weapon. Maybe Dominic and Scooter would even question what she intended to do and who Tammy intended to kill with the gun. Worse, Dominic and Scooter could take the weapon from her leaving Tammy with no way to kill them. No, it was best to play the ace card last and produce the gun when it was least expected.

The second time Tammy wanted to pull the gun from behind her back was when Dominic pointed the gun at her head in the basement and threatened Tammy to go down the tunnel ahead of them. Tammy didn't appreciate being threatened, and the same feeling of helplessness she experienced back in the hotel when Cross invited others in on the murder of her husband overcame her now. At least this time, not only did Dominic underestimate the four people he was pursuing, but he also was underestimating Tammy.

Tammy almost produced the gun a third time was when the creatures attacked them in the basement. Tammy had placed her hand behind her back and clutched the gun grip, ready to pull the weapon out if it was needed. It turned out not to be necessary as Dominic and Scooter were both capable of dispatching the creatures with minimal effort.

Now she was traversing the tunnel of shit, the gun firmly behind her back. She turned, and the light from Scooter's flashlight was no longer visible. Ahead of her, Tammy could finally see the tunnel emptying into a more extensive cavern and, upon reaching the bigger cavern, saw two men struggling on the ground. Dominic had a knife in his hand while Jason was kicking at Dominic's head, trying to escape the coming attack. Tammy reached for the gun hidden behind her back and hesitated. It would be better if Dominic killed Jason. After the task of killing Jason was complete, Tammy would still need Dominic to eliminate Jason's friends the other witnesses who could implicate her. Best to wait, she thought as she watched the two men wrestle from the tunnel.

Instead of Dominic killing Jason, what Tammy witnessed was unspeakable. Jason was fighting back, and after kicking Dominic in the face, Jason got up and ran into the left-most tunnel. When Dominic got up, pistol in hand, he ran to the same tunnel and pointed his gun into the tunnel, firing three times. Dominic peered into the tunnel and was about to give chase but elected to fire two more shots into the tunnel for good measure instead.

Dominic was listening for any sounds when Tammy tapped him on the shoulder. The adrenaline was pumping through Dominic's body was pumping hard, and Tammy could see nothing other than blood in his eyes.

"Did you hit him?" Tammy asked for some reason holding her gun in her hand behind her back.

"I don't know. I don't think so." Dominic said, trying to process everything and calm down.

"We should go after him. We shouldn't let him get away." Tammy said quietly, soothing Dominic with her voice and taking her hand off her gun, as she turned and dug through the floor of shit and picking up the flashlight Dominic had dropped when Jason struck him on the head with the rock. Tammy then handed the flashlight to Dominic, giving her approval to continue the chase.

Needing no further invitation to proceed after his quarry, Dominic shined the flashlight down the tunnel before following after Jason. After traveling about twenty-five yards, Tammy saw Dominic start to lose his cool. He had expelled five bullets down a narrow tunnel, and there was nothing, no corpse, no Jason, and no blood. But the shit they were walking on had finally come to an end, and rock became the new floor bottom once again. However, smell-wise, it no longer mattered, as both Tammy and Dominic were covered in feces from head to toe.

Going down the left tunnel was much shorter in duration than the tunnel of feces they previously traversed. While the tunnel of excrement felt like it was multiple football fields long. After about thirty or forty yards, the rock floor appeared beneath them, and a second smaller cavern opened up as the tunnel they were currently in ended. Dominic took no chances this time and was prepared for an ambush as he approached this open cavern and moved the flashlight along the walls checking for Jason and, seeing no signs of danger, stepped out into the small cavern.

The open cavern was similar to the large room of shit they were just in, only this room was smaller in circumference and again opened to a left tunnel and a right tunnel ahead of them. Above them, the room stretched to fifteen feet to the ceiling. Jason could have exited down either tunnel. Tammy and Dominic had no way of knowing which way Jason fled.

Tammy stepped out of the tunnel. Before reaching a decision on which tunnel Jason could have gone down, the decision was made for them. In the left tunnel, two creatures appeared. One in front of the other. Tammy held her breath, not wanting to see them and wishing they would just go away.

Dominic raised up his gun and fired into the creatures before they could attack him. Dominic shot at the first albino creature, striking the first creature twice as the figure dropped dead ahead of its counterpart. The second creature moved around its now dead twin and stepped over him. Dominic pulled the trigger twice more and heard the empty clicks of the gun as the gun was no longer in possession of any ammunition.

Dropping the pistol to the ground, Dominic pulled the knife from his waistband and readied himself for the upcoming attack. Behind him, three shots rang out, and the creature before him stopped and dropping to the floor dead. Dominic turned with the flashlight and looked at Tammy holding the gun.

"Where did you get that?" Dominic asked about the gun.

"You don't honestly believe I would come down here unarmed, do you?" Tammy retorted.

The two stood there squared off, standing with about a foot and a half in distance between them. Dirt, dust, and shit floated in the air, illuminated by the flashlight Cross had. Cross, holding the flashlight and the knife while Tammy was holding the gun. The pair of former lovers stood feet apart, staring at one another, both thinking unspoken words. Tammy didn't want things to end like this for Dominic, not yet.

"I just saved you." Tammy said.

"But you didn't trust me." Dominic said, and truthfully, looking at Tammy, he knew she would never trust him.

"Look." Tammy said under her breath, pointing the gun at the same tunnel as two more creatures emerged, crawling over their dead counterparts.

Dominic dropped the flashlight, and it rolled on the ground. More albino creatures appeared behind the two coming up the tunnel towards them this time. The first two creatures that emerged grabbed hold of the first dead creature's dead body and pulled it back into the tunnel. The albino cave dwellers who crawled behind them started to push into the open cavern towards Dominic and Tammy.

Dominic turned and brought the knife up, facing them. Then as Tammy started to raise her gun, Dominic did something unexpected. Dominic turned towards Tammy and placed his free hand on the back of Tammy's head and placed his lips on Tammy's lips and kissed her with passion.

Then there was a sharp pain in Tammy's stomach, and when she tried to back away, she was held in place by Dominic's kiss and the strength of his hand on the back of her neck. The warmth started to ooze from her stomach as Dominic pulled the knife out of her abdomen. He then clutched her in his arms, so she could not raise and point the gun at him.

"I love you." Dominic whispered to her in her ear.

They both remained standing, at another time or place the couple could have been mistaken as romantically dancing while entangled with one another. Dominic was trying to maneuver the gun away from Tammy's grasp. Although she was bleeding from being stabbed in the abdomen, Tammy would not relinquish to Dominic. She fired the pistol at the ground three times. The creatures from the tunnel were closing in on the pair of them. Dominic pushed the still breathing Tammy away from his embrace and into the onslaught of albino creatures coming at them.

Tammy grabbed her belly as she was pushed away and tried to scream but found no words coming from her throat. She clutched the gun and tried raising her arm to point it at Dominic but could not squeeze the trigger as there were too many claw-like hands clutching at her from behind. The cave dwellers began tearing into her and dragging her away, and then the lights of her eyes were starting to drift away. As Tammy was dragged into the tunnel, into the darkness of death, the albino attackers took turns eating on her flesh one painful bite at a time.

After feeding Tammy to the creatures, Dominic did not wait around to watch or say goodbye. Using the diversion he created, Dominic grabbed the flashlight he had dropped off the floor and, with the knife in hand, proceeded down the right-side tunnel after Jason Matthews. Cross would never feel guilty or sad about leading Tammy, his ex-lover, to her death. At that moment, Cross only had one thought to catch up with Jason Matthews.

26 – Abrams

Abrams led Marcus and Brooke through the tunnel on the right side. Abrams hated the idea of leaving Jason behind, but deep inside, he was aware Jason was correct. The group could not fight off killers with guns behind them while fighting off the creatures who resided in these tunnels in front of them. Whatever Jason was planning on doing, Abrams wished Jason the best of luck. But being a realist, Abrams did not hold out much hope for Jason's success.

After minutes of traveling down the right-side tunnel, two things happened in succession. The first was the mounds of feces they had been traveling on disappeared, and the ground turned to rock, replacing the shit on the floor, making the landscape of the tunnel easier to navigate. The second was the gunshots they heard behind them, most likely in the small cavern they had left minutes before. The gunshots were in succession, multiple rounds, leaving little doubt the shots were fired at the location where they had left Jason Matthews.

If the creatures were attracted to sound, those gunshots would attract their attention, a lot of their attention. Without having to tell his companions anything, they pressed on. If Jason died allowing them to gain some time and ground, it was best not to waste the opportunity. Moving on for another forty minutes or so, the tunnel they were in opened up to another small cavern. The circumference of the new cavern was three times bigger than the last cavern of shit they had been in and was about forty feet around. But once again, the cavern was about fifteen feet tall, allowing the group to stand up and stretch their legs. Instead of there being only two tunnels to choose from, there were now six. It was folly to try and guess which tunnel led outside or how much longer the tunnels could be.

"The place is one giant labyrinth." Abrams said.

"I need a chance to rest." Marcus said, no longer keeping his face covered with the vest, but still holding the injured side of his face with the blood-stained vest. Brooke helped Marcus to the ground, and Marcus sat taking a break catching his breath.

"I know what these creatures are. They are humans like us. At least, in theory, they are as human as we are." Marcus said after waiting five or six breathes.

"Excuse me, what do you mean they're human?" Abrams softly tried to keep his voice down as he kept the flashlight on the six tunnels before them.

"They are us. These albinos are human like us. The same genes, the same chromosomes, and most of the same traits" Marcus repeated.

"Those monsters are not human; they look nothing like us." Brooke said.

"The newspaper article said slaves were brought down into the basement and executed. The paper also said when the authorities showed up, they could hear the howls and screams of several slaves running around these caves and made no attempts to rescue them." Marcus said.

"So, these are former slaves? Bullshit." Abrams said, getting unintentionally louder.

"Do you know who Charles Darwin is?" Marcus asked, looking up at Abrams.

"Yes, the theory of evolution." Brooke said.

"And what is evolution? Simply summed up, evolution is man rising from the sea and over millions of years transforming into a monkey and from a monkey into a human being, right?" Marcus said, looking for agreement from Brooke and Abrams.

"Wrong." Marcus corrected them. "Darwin never said that we as humans evolved from Monkeys. It is a common misinterpretation that he even suggested that we evolved from monkeys. Darwin did suggest we shared a common ancestor. Darwin was more interested in Natural Selection. In fact, his book is not titled, On the Origin of Species. It is titled On the Origin of Species by Means of Natural Selection." Marcus said, closing his eyes.

"What's the difference between Natural Selection and Evolution?" Abrams asked.

"Evolution is a component, perhaps the key component of Natural Selection. But Natural Selection is the passing on of certain traits or characteristics to offspring. Essentially, all organisms pass on traits, mutations, genes, and characteristics. Some characteristics or traits tend to do better in certain environments. Those organisms with traits that do better in certain environments tend to be more successful at reproducing and therefore, multiplying and spreading those traits." Marcus said.

"So essentially, the environment favors one set of traits to reproduce over another." Brooke said following the conversation.

"Simply said, when Natural Selection occurs, it means one set of traits is favored by the environment over another set of traits. Those species exhibiting the traits favored by the environment tend to become the dominant set of traits in that species. Those which are not favored tend to not be as likely to be passed on."

"I suppose this happens in nature all the time?" Abrams said, still unconvinced.

"No, it is actually an infrequent occurrence, but it has been known to happen in bacteria. Darwin noted it in the finches he studied at the Galapagos Islands and moths during the industrial revolution. But there has been a recent example of Natural Selection in the elephants in Africa." Marcus said.

"Elephants? You are comparing elephants with these things running around down here eating people?" Abrams said

"In Africa, elephants with tusks are considered very valuable to trophy hunters who kill them just to take their tusks. But were you aware, there is a breed of elephant in Africa that does not have a tusk? Most recently, this breed of elephant has overtaken those with elephants with tusks in terms of population. Trophy hunters do not kill tusk-less elephants because they don't have any ivory. Therefore, elephants without tusks have become more successful at mating. The trait of not having tusks is being passed on and is now the predominant trait amongst the elephant species." Marcus said.

"Now imagine, fifty or sixty maybe even a hundred slaves are driven down to the cavern and in here. They breed and have sexual relations with one another. Let me ask you, which traits would a person need to grow up, survive, catch food, or hunt in such an environment of caves like these long term? Better hearing. Better eyesight. A better sense of smell to find their prey, stronger legs to catch their prey, outside in the world taller is better, but conversely

136

down here being smaller could be considered optimal to traverse through the tunnels. Those with traits for certain immunities or against certain diseases would be favored through reproduction." Marcus continued.

"Now strip away all that makes a human being, speech, clothing, being clean or sanitary and give us long nails to claw and kill our prey or dig new tunnels or even stronger teeth so they could tear into flesh." Marcus said, feeling the side of his face with the missing ear.

"Okay. Let's say I buy into this theory that the monsters are us. How long would this Natural Selection take to affect these creatures?" Abrams asked.

"The newspaper, Jason and I found said they were brought down here in eighteen sixty-five, that is almost one hundred and fifty-six years ago. Today, an average human being could expect to live sixty to seventy years, which would be two to three generations. However, with these creatures, I would guess their life span is much less than ours. Maybe, they live to be twenty or thirty years old. Given their lack of access to medicine, sanitation, and food. It could be seven to ten generations of these things affected by Natural Selection and having key traits passed on. Traits which we find unimportant passed on as key traits for their survival becoming more dominant." Marcus said.

"Alright, story time is over. We need to get moving." Abrams said as he bent to pick Marcus up off the floor.

"But what about their language? Did they just forget how to talk one day?" Brooke asked.

"Who says they don't communicate with one another. Maybe it's through snarls, grunts, growls, or even clicks of the tongue. Some of the tribes in Botswana and Namibia located in Africa use a Khoisan language of clicking sounds in their language. It might not be so far-fetched to believe even the length, tone, or duration of certain growls or snarls could stand for different things." Marcus said as he looked ahead at the tunnels to his left and became paralyzed with fear.

Abrams, with the flashlight, picked up on Marcus, shutting his mouth quickly, turned, and saw one of the creatures staring directly at him in the third tunnel. The creature was unmoving, sitting back on its hind legs, getting ready to pounce on their group.

137

Seeing the creature, Abrams let out a breath, and the creature charged in his direction. Firing a single shot from the gun, Abrams hit the creature directly in the center of its chest, dropping the albino creature a few steps before it could reach them. Abrams kept his gun on the dead cave dweller lying on the floor, shining the light on it to ensure it was killed. As Abrams turned to say something to Brooke and Marcus, a second creature unseen by anyone jumped on Abrams. The albino attacker took Abrams gun hand into its own claw-like hands and Abrams bicep in its other hand. With Abrams pistol arm fully extended, Abrams was desperately attempting to free his captured hand. Struggling, trying to pull his arm back away from the creature proved fruitless, and with a firm grip, the creature chomped down on Abrams's wrist.

A scream filled the tunnel system with Abrams yelling in pain. Abrams dropped to his knees before the creature, releasing the flashlight and gun from both his hands.

Brooke picked up the flashlight and, using it like a baseball bat, striking the creature whose mouth was attached to Abrams's wrist on the side of its head. The flashlight cracked, and the glass lens shattered onto the floor. The light from the flashlight was no longer working. The distraction worked as the creature stopped chewing on Abrams' wrist. Slowly releasing its grip on Abrams's arm to turn its attention towards Brooke. Brooke, to her credit, did not back down and stood with the broken flashlight cocked back in her arms off to her side, ready to swing when the creature decided to attack her.

Marcus, perhaps thinking more clearly, picked up the gun Abrams dropped. Placing his left hand on Abrams' mouth to prevent him from screaming any further shot the creature in the kneecap as its attention was turned toward Brooke.

Being shot in the knee, the creature howled in pain, losing all interest in Brooke. The albino attacker fell on the ground and began crying and yelling as it held its bloodied knee in its claw-like fingered hands.

"I am taking my hand off of your mouth. Do not under any circumstances scream or make any noise." Marcus whispered into Abrams' ear.

Abrams looked at his wrist, which the creature had bitten into. Blood spurted into the air, and Abrams felt as if he would pass out. His left hand held the dangling right hand into place as the right hand flopped about at the wrist. A giant chunk of Abrams' wrist was missing.

Marcus pulled his belt off his jeans and took Abrams' right arm into his lap, placing a tourniquet onto Abrams' forearm underneath his elbow. After placing the tourniquet on Abrams, he held Abrams' arm over his head into the air, attempting to keep the blood flow from leaving Abrams' body.

"If you want any chance of surviving this, you need to keep your arm up in the air." Marcus said to Abrams and placed the vest he was using to cover his face tied around the bite wound to try and stop the bleeding.

Turning around, Marcus saw three more creatures emerge from the tunnels on their side. The creature's attention was centered on the screaming creature holding its knee on the ground in pain. Grabbing Brooke by the mouth from behind, Marcus guided her into one of the tunnels on the opposite side. Marcus then bent and assisted Abrams up onto his feet, keeping his arm in the air and placing Abrams into the same tunnel behind Brooke. Marcus took another look behind him as the three creatures jumped the injured creature he had shot in the knee cap. Marcus briefly watched as the villains cannibalized their own weakened compatriot before fleeing into the tunnel behind Abrams and Brooke.

Brooke still held the broken flashlight in her hand, leading the way as they passed through the tunnel. Abrams was moving considerably slower since the attack on his hand.

"Don't look at your arm. Just try and keep your arm up in the air." Marcus said, trying to help Abrams pick up the pace.

"You may as well get rid of the gun. You used the last of the bullets to shoot that thing." Abrams said, grimacing in pain.

Marcus wasn't so sure Abrams was correct about being out of bullets. He didn't know anything about guns but put the gun into his back pocket just in case.

"Why didn't they attack us?" Brooke, hearing conversation behind her, asked.

"They are attracted by movement, but more than movement, they are attracted to sound. Cries, voices, gunshots, walking, maybe even breathing will draw them down on you. Knowing that the kneecap is one of the most painful areas a person can injure, I rightly believed an injury to the creature's kneecap would cause him to holler and cry in pain. So, I shot the creature in the knee to provide us with a chance of escape. The other creatures could not help passing up on a free meal, even if it was one of their own." Marcus said.

"What do we do now?" Brooke said.

"Pray we can find an exit soon." Marcus said, looking at Abrams, who had become visibly paler even in the dark.

Part Three: Ending

27 – Scooter

Scooter resumed his crawl at a slow pace through the tunnel. His progress further impeded as he moved along the floor of feces that stuck into his hands, clothing, and hair. To add to his exhaustion and size hindrance, Scooter also became nauseous from the smell. Scooter became sick, throwing up and unable to control his bowels began defecating in his pants. Pieces of shit from the floor of the tunnel became embedded into his pointy beard. Scooter needed to decide, continue forward through the shit tunnel or turn back towards safety.

Scooter became genuinely afraid, not of the creatures which had attacked him and Dominic earlier but of the tight space he found himself in. Claustrophobia. He wanted to turn around, go back out through the tunnels and into the house, go back to the motel, take a shower, and forget this had ever happened. As far as bad days go, this may have topped the list as far as Scooter was concerned. While he wanted to support Dominic, get the money and avenge Melinda, things changed when the monsters appeared, and he started chasing people through tunnels of shit.

But as bad as things went, Scooter continued forward. He considered Dominic his best friend and brother. They shared a bond that only being in prison could formulate together. Scooter continued his slow pace through the tunnel floor of feces, handful by handful. Finally, after what seemed an eternity, Scooter reached the first large room, the room where Dominic Cross had been attacked by one camouflaged feces-covered Jason Matthews in the dark with a rock.

Being able to stand up was the first natural feeling of relief Scooter had felt. Stretching his legs and his back, Scooter wiped the sweat from his face as carefully as he was able to, trying not to smear any more feces onto his face or beard. There were two tunnels before him, one to the left and one to the right. Which tunnel should Scooter consider taking? Doubts and bad feelings start plaguing Scooter's mind. Thoughts he deemed to be bad juju. Scooter was ready to turn himself around and make his way back to the vehicles to head home with or with Dominic Cross.

Scooter kept thinking the only option was going back the way he came in through the tunnel. In the left tunnel, gunfire rang out, a flurry of shots rang out in succession. Dominic shined his flashlight in the direction down the tunnel. The gunshots Scooter heard did not seem to be far away. Dominic could be hurt or in need of his help, Scooter thought. Dominic may have killed them.

One more tunnel, Scooter thought to himself, just to see what was up ahead, see what's being shot at, and if Dominic needs his help, otherwise I'll turn around. So, Scooter crouched back down into the feces covering the floor and started down the left tunnel towards the gunshots.

Thankfully, after a few yards, the feces on the floor had stopped, and the ground became rock solid again. The hard surface was worse on the big man's knees. It still was better than crawling through shit, Scooter thought. After crawling about forty or fifty more yards at a snail's pace, Scooter came into another smaller cavern he was able to stand up in. This cavern was close in size to the one he could stand up in previously and another opportunity to take a break. Taking the flashlight beam around the cavern, Scooter noticed the unmistakable puddles of blood that lead into the cavern on the left. It wasn't just a trickle of blood; it was liters of blood skidded on the ground of a person or persons being dragged down into the tunnel.

Shining his light into the left tunnel where the blood was visible, he saw several tiny eyes peering back at him. Scooter was unsure precisely what he was seeing and at first moved closer with the flashlight, then, becoming afraid, backed away and had decided to flee back into the tunnel of shit from which he had just come through.

As he reached the entrance to the tunnel and was preparing to get in, four creatures came up from the left tunnel behind him and started to bite and claw at him. These creatures did not have the size, coordination, or strength of the creatures he and Dominic had fought earlier in the more giant cavern. These creatures stood about two feet to two and a half feet tall and weighed twenty to thirty pounds each. They may have been the offspring of the adult's creatures, but they moved just as quick.

The first of the smaller creatures to reach Scooter bit into his back calf through his jeans. Scooter yelped in pain. The bite was worse than being bit by a dog, and Scooter turned around and kicked at the small creature with his boot. Another creature bit Scooter in the thigh, and Scooter back-handed the beast with the flashlight and, having had enough of the pain, removed the small T-Ball bat from the metal chain on his waist.

A third small creature tried to bite Scooter through his boot. Feeling the pressure in the leather of his boot against his skin, Scooter stepped on the creature's back, removed his foot from the tiny creature's grasp, and proceeded to step repeatedly on the back of the creature's head, squishing until blood poured from the creatures' eyes and mouth. The next smaller creature to attack Scooter tried running up toward Scooter from the front, and Scooter taking advantage of size and being able to stand up entirely in the grotto, bent at the knees and took aim and striking the T-Ball bat square on the creature's cranium. The albino offspring hit the back wall and slumped to the floor; the life sucked out of him.

The next creature attempted to jump at Scooter and slashed at Scooter's shirt and face with its claw-like fingers. Scooter dropped the flashlight on the floor and watched as the light rolled along the rock floor. Scooter using the T-Ball bat, pulled the legs of the creature out from underneath the albino. Then reaching down on the floor, Scooter grabbed the struggling albino child by the legs and began swinging the creature into the wall of the cavern. The tiny creature smashed on the rock wall repeatedly until Scooter's arms became tired, and there was nothing left of what he was holding but bloody stumps. Blood smeared the wall of the cavern where the creature's body repeatedly hit. Tired, Scooter took a step back in victory and looked at the bodies lying on the floor. Picking up the flashlight and T-Ball bat. Scooter still had the gun tucked away into his belt but hadn't needed to use the firearm against smaller foes.

As he took a breath in, he thought to himself, is that it? Is that the best these creatures have to offer? His mood changed when a full-sized albino creature appeared in the same tunnel these smaller ones had emerged from. This creature stood about four to four and a half feet tall, and while Scooter had a size and strength advantage on the beast, Scooter was also tired from the fighting and crawling.

The creature approached out of the tunnel and sprung towards Scooter. Scooter's right hand was on the T-Ball bat, and as the albino closed in on Scooter, he swung the T-Ball bat. The creature's claws had just reached into Scooter's abdomen as the T-Ball bat connected with the creature's head. The full-sized albino cave dweller staggered but remained on his feet. This creature was not as easy to dispose of as the smaller ones, and the beast turned, repositioning itself to attack Scooter again. Scooter, tired and in pain from the last few assaults, elected to drop the T-Ball bat and produce the hang gun from his waist. He fired four times, each time taking a step back until Scooter's back was pressed against the wall. Despite being a small area, Scooter fired and missed the first two shots until he connected on the third round, wounding the creature. The wound did not stop the beast from pressing forward. Firing the fourth round, Scooter was able to punch the ticket of the full-sized albino, striking the wounded cave dweller in the chest as Scooter watched the creature crane over and fall down face first.

Scooter had a strong sense of self-preservation. While he didn't want to let Dominic down and loved Melinda, Scooter decided to halt proceeding further. He was on his last few rounds of ammunition and did not want to die down here looking for fool's gold. Placing the gun back into his belt, Scooter being careful to avoid the body of the full-sized creature he had just killed, once again picked up the flashlight and the T-Ball bat and started his crawl back in the tunnel back towards the tunnel of feces and the exit.

Going on pure adrenaline and fright, Scooter made better time crawling through the first forty yards the second time than he did the first. He could visualize the exit, the fresh air, and most of all, the open spaces once he was out. Getting to safety was Scooter's only thought. Thinking of fresh air and safety made Scooter less anxious traveling and provided Scooter with a positive image to strive for. These thoughts stayed with Scooter until he started crawling back through the feces-covered floor for a second time.

If crawling through the feces the first time was terrible, the second time was not as horrendous. Scooter crawled on all fours, he was already covered in filth from the previous experience through the tunnel, and he never actually stopped smelling the shit even when he was finished crawling through the feces before. At least this time, Scooter could estimate how much further he needed to crawl to exit the tunnels and subterranean levels. It was not long before Scooter was back in the larger room of shit. One last tunnel to get through, he thought, the longest one.

Scooter decided a slight breather would be beneficial before starting the long trek back down the first tunnel. This would be Scooter's last time to stand and stretch his legs. Behind him, though, he could hear a noise, a clawing or scraping in the tunnel he had just emerged from. Scooter holstered the T-Ball bat on his waist and pulled out the handgun. Keeping the gun pointed at the tunnel behind him, and without taking a much-needed break, Scooter proceeded back into the first tunnel he was in initially trying to keep escape.

Crawling forward through the feces, Scooter kept stopping and pointing the flashlight behind him to see if any of those creatures were following. Perspiration, dirt, and shit clouded his vision in the dark, and his breathing became so rapid his heart pumped loudly in his chest. "Stop, he told his heart, keep quiet. They will hear you." Scooter said to himself and his heart. Nonetheless, his pulse quickened, and so did the number of times; Scooter stopped to look behind him with the flashlight to see if there were any creatures in pursuit.

Each time Scooter looked, there was nothing there as he slushed through the masses of feces. Then Scooter heard another noise, this time from up ahead of him, in front of him. Raising the flashlight forward, he saw one of the creatures ahead of him, sitting in the tunnel looking with its vacant eyes directly at him. At first, the creature just stared and then smelled and then proceeded to come after Scooter.

Scooter pointed the handgun and fired three times, striking the creature dead. Now the tricky part, as his breathing increased, Scooter needed to navigate his way past the creature's dead body. The tunnel was barely big enough for Scooter to navigate through with no obstacles, add in a carcass of about one hundred pounds and make that one hundred pounds a terrorizing flesh-eating creature. There was enough to keep Scooter paralyzed with fear and slow his progress.

Scooter started his slow pass by of the creature's dead body by pushing on the dead creature's head and face with the barrel of the gun to see if the albino would move. The creature's pale white eyes remained open but unmoving. Deciding the cave dweller was dead, Scooter's body pressed tightly on the carcass of the dead creature, their bodies hugging as Scooter moved past the dead creature's head and claw-like hands, its unbreathing, unflinching ribcage and then the creature's genitals. Scooter was trying hard not to stare at the creature's sex organs and had almost made his way past the creature's dead body when Scooter's foot became stuck.

Scooter tried to kick his footloose and struggled to move forward. He then felt a sharp pain in the same calf where the smaller creature had bitten him earlier. Scooter yelled out and grimaced. Shining the light back behind him, Scooter saw another creature standing over his feet, feeding on his leg. In pain and now going through visible shock, Scooter pointed the handgun behind him and, while laying in shit and on top of a dead creature, fired the gun three times.

Scooter hit the creature once in the shoulder, forcing the albino attacker to retreat at least temporarily. The second bullet missed and hit the tunnel's ceiling, and with the third bullet, Scooter had shot himself in the foot. Scooter yelled out in pain a second time. Tears flowed from his eyes, and his mouth became an oasis of drool as he cried in pain.

Scooter began striking the wall with his fists in anger. How could he be so stupid as to shoot himself in the foot? After releasing the anger, Scooter had no choice but to continue to crawl, this time not on all four limbs, as his right leg was seriously injured from being used as a meal and for target practice. Unable to use his leg, Scooter used only his upper body strength to push himself and crawl forward. He had physically exhausted himself after only a few yards of going forward. Behind him, Scooter started to hear noises again. In a panic, Scooter pointed the flashlight behind him. He could see the creature he had shot in the shoulder coming forward towards him.

Gulping with his heart in his throat, sweat running into his eyes, and not being able to breathe, Scooter was taking aim with the gun, and ahead of him in the tunnel, he could hear a snarl, moving the flashlight towards his head, he could see another creature coming his way. Two full-size albino creatures were coming from two different directions. He was boxed in from the front and the

147

back. Thoughts of suicide ran through Scooter's mind, one bullet under his chin, and there would be no more pain.

Scooter started praying out loud, "Hail Mary, full of grace the Lord is with thee. Oh, fuck it." He stopped himself, he never considered himself very religious before, and there would be no mercy for him now, Scooter thought.

Scooter changed his mind about committing suicide as the creatures approached. If he was going down, he would go down swinging. Scooter had never known another way; he had always been a fighter. If they wanted a piece of him, he would take equal amounts of flesh from them. He turned and pointed the gun toward the creature from ahead of him and pulled the trigger twice. Two bullets, both striking their target, and Scooter watched as the creature in front of him fell dead.

Retaking his aim, he pointed the gun at the wounded albino creature behind him, who was grabbing for Scooter's feet and his bloody boot. Scooter again pulled the trigger of the weapon, and this time there was an empty clicking sound as the gun was out of bullets. Scooter tried to throw the empty gun at the creature. As the wounded albino took hold of Scooter's leg, a second albino came beside him and grabbed Scooter's foot. Instead of eating him there, the creatures pulled Scooter back over the dead carcass he was laying on and back through the tunnel of shit as Scooter kicked and screamed in terror.

Scooter tried to use his hands to find a place to hold onto in the feces or the walls. He attempted to kick at the creatures, trying and wiggle free from their grasp, but these strategies proved useless. The hairless albino creatures dragged Scooter back through the tunnel and into the larger room of feces. As Scooter attempted to pull his T-Ball bat from his belt and stand up to fight, two other creatures already in the room joined the creatures which had dragged. Before Scooter could do anything to defend himself, the four creatures began to feast. The fleshy parts of Scooter's underarms and his triceps. His stomach and his thighs. Scooter could only flail around, attempting to push them off and punching them from the ground as he tried to grab at the T-Ball bat. Scooter would not die a quick death. He suffered many missing chunks of flesh, numerous bites, and an extraordinary amount of blood loss before Scooter would stop struggling. Scooter took a knee for a final time before the creatures fell on top of him.

28 - Jason Matthews

Covered in shit, Jason Matthews narrowly escaped the knife attack brought on by Dominic Cross, and after kicking Cross in the face, Jason Matthews started for the tunnel on the left. "Lead him away and give Marcus and the others a chance." Jason thought to himself. Then as he started down the tunnel, the sound of bullets rang out behind him. Three loud bangs in succession. Jason dove to the ground of feces and, laying in shit, realized he needed to get up and move quickly.

Jason started by belly crawling, keeping his body as close to the ground as possible. More gunshots rang down the tunnel from behind him, some of the bullets striking the ceiling tunnel above him dropping rock pebbles on his face and body. This time covering his head and face, Jason dropped the phone Abrams had given him. After waiting a few seconds with no further gunshots, Jason got up and began crawling on all four limbs after picking up Abrams' cell phone and stashing the phone in his back pocket. Realizing time was of the essence before Dominic Cross would follow after him, Jason crawled on all four limbs in a hurry.

If there were more gunshots in his direction, he would be a sitting duck, as the tunnel proceeded straight away with no opportunities for cover. So far, all the missed bullets had been complete luck or poorly aimed shots hitting the walls or the ceiling around him. Jason thought to himself, it was better to get shot in the ass than in the head if he was crouch walking. Moving as quickly as he could, Jason completed the forty or fifty yards when another small cavern opened up ahead of him.

Upon entering the next small cavern, there were again two tunnels in front of him, a left tunnel and a right tunnel. Jason chooses the right-side tunnel without wasting time debating which of the two tunnels he should take or stopping to take a breath or break. Jason felt he needed to put some distance between him and the man pursuing him. Now moving back to a crouch walk, Jason navigated the rightmost tunnel. Not slowing up, he hoped his purser would incorrectly choose the opposite tunnel from him and miss him entirely.

Less than what felt like two minutes later, Jason heard gunshots, several of them, ringing out in succession behind him. This time Jason did stop and look behind him. The gunshots were not aimed at him. They were back in the small cavern Jason had hurried through. Had he caught a break? Perhaps his attackers were in conflict with more of those creatures. Maybe he would get lucky, and they would be killed. Jason resumed his travels in the darkness of the tunnel.

After traveling for what felt to be about thirty minutes, exhaustion had started to set. Jason's legs were beginning to cramp, and the adrenaline faded. Just when things began to feel bleak again, the tunnel opened into another cavern before him. He went through the opening of the grotto and saw before him two more tunnels. "Does this place ever end?" Jason thought to himself. But before choosing a tunnel to go into, Jason stood up briefly to stretch his legs. In the darkness running across the cave floor, Jason tripped, taking a misstep on a series of rocks, and hit his head as he landed on the floor.

For just a brief moment, Jason lost consciousness. All was black. As Jason's eyes closed, and with a throbbing in his head, Jason thought he could hear a voice speaking to him

"Get up, Jason. Wake up, Jason." The female voice was familiar. The voice was soft, begging him to stir. Causing Jason to wake from his daze. Still groggy from the tap on his head, the voice grew stronger, calling for Jason to get up. Jason recognized the voice as his wife Tammy's voice.

"Why?" Jason muttered in the empty cavern to himself as he was half unconscious.

"Why did you betray me? Betray us?" He said out loud in the cavern, speaking to Tammy's voice.

"You only need to get up now and look above you." Tammy said, her voice fading away.

Jason rolled over on the stones, his back lying flat on the ground as his eyes fumbled to open. He knew there was an urgency. But in his stupor, Jason could not recall what the urgency was at this moment to hurry. All feelings of danger he felt had temporarily disappeared and were gone. A nice deep sleep was so much more appealing.

"Jason, you need to look above you, but you need to open your eyes now." The voice of Tammy said to him one last time before leaving him permanently.

Startled, Jason opened his eyes. His eyes adjusted in the darkness. Lying on his back in a cold sweat, he looked up to the ceiling above him. The top above was not like the ceiling of the other caverns he had stopped in. In this cave, the roof was much closer to his actual height and as tall.

The size of the cavern was not the only noticeable difference. Nearest, the right-side tunnel located on the cavern's far wall was a slight incline mound. The mound was almost at a forty-five-degree angle connecting the floor and the wall. Looking up at the ceiling above the incline mound was an opening in the dirt above. Jason could see moonlight breaking through the gap. Not bright lights, but the light emanating from a moon or stars, and more importantly, there was fresh air.

Dangling down from the opening in the ceiling was grass and roots from the trees above. The space was about three feet wide, more than enough to squeeze through if he could pull himself up and out of the cavern. Jason, now standing up on his feet, walked up the incline. Digging his feet into the grooves carved into the rock, Jason could climb up the opening where the cavern met the outside. The angle of the dirt mound and indents in the walls were not naturally occurring features of the cave. Most likely, Jason concluded they had been dug by the creatures using the wall to reach the outside, so they could search for food and water. He dug his feet into the grooves and began climbing up using the holes to place his hands. After using two of the holes to steady himself and about two feet off the incline mound, Jason reached the roots above him. Using the roots of the tree, Jason began pulling himself up through the hole.

After sticking his body up through the hole, he pulled his feet clear of the tunnel. Exiting the tunnel system, Jason was now outside in the dark in a copse of trees in a forest. Kneeling with both hands on his knees, Jason took a deep smell of fresh air and momentarily began to cry, dropping on his hands in front of his face. A small victory, Jason thought to escape the labyrinth below.

Looking to his left and right to see if there were any landmarks and where he was, Jason realized the forest ended through a thin line of two or three rows of trees to his left. After the trees was an open field, and in the distance, he could see the outline of the Walnford house standing in the moonlight. All of the traveling underground, what felt like miles and hours of crouching and crawling, and Jason had gone less than two hundred yards from the front porch where his adventure had started.

Next to Jason, there was the sound of rock and scurrying from the hole Jason had just pulled himself through. Looking down below, the man who held him at gunpoint appeared to be climbing up the exact notches in the wall Jason had used to exit the cavern. He would be up outside the hole in a few moments. Jason had two options, fight here when the man finished climbing up the hole and hope to take advantage of his foe's weariness, or run and avoid the fight.

With his hands on his knees still, Jason felt something in his pocket, the car key fob. Although the car had been disabled by the woman working with his adversaries, Jason had an idea. The idea was crazy, but could the plan work? Jason looked at the Walnford household in the distance, and picking himself off the ground, ran through the tree line and into the open field. Running back to the disabled car parked in front of the Walnford house.

29 - Dominic Cross

Cross came out of the tunnel into the small cavern. Cross saw Jason Matthews climbing the wall next to the right tunnel and pulling himself out through a hole in the ceiling in the corner of the cave. Cross had missed catching up with Jason Matthews by a matter of seconds. Undeterred, Cross stashed the knife in his belt and, in the dark, started up the incline mound to continue the chase.

Finding the notches in the wall and using the same roots Jason had just used, Cross pulled himself up through the hole. Cross was careful exiting through the hole above, being aware that he could be vulnerable to attack once he reached the top of the exit. Upon reaching the top and pulling his head out of the ground, he peered out, and not seeing any sign of Jason Matthews, Cross pulled himself entirely out of the hole and exited the tunnel system.

Finding himself in the woods, Cross did not stop to take a breath or relax or thank God as Jason had done a few moments before. Rolling onto his stomach, he propped himself up onto his feet and began looking through the trees for Jason Matthews. In the moonlight, Cross could see the outline of the main house of the Walnford Plantation. He could see Jason Matthews running a few yards ahead of him through an open field toward the house. Dominic Cross resumed his pursuit with an unnerving smile on his face.

Dominic's one thought as he ran after Jason was, once Cross caught him, he would cut Jason Matthews into pieces slowly and feed him to one of those fucking albino creatures. Jason started with a sixty- or seventy-yard head start, but Dominic was gaining on him, and running faster would overtake him shortly. Moving at a much quicker pace than his adversary and keeping his eyes on him, Dominic saw Jason run to the front of the house and then take something out of his pocket and point the object at his vehicle.

That was unexpected, Dominic said to himself as he watched Jason point the key fob at the car and saw the trunk open. Closing in at about fifty yards away, Cross saw Jason climb inside the car's trunk area and shut himself inside the compartment.

Why would he do that? Dominic asked himself, slowing his pursuit. Did Jason not think Dominic saw him climb in the trunk? Jason had no more avenues of escape and no more places to hide. Locking himself into the trunk of the vehicle, Jason had essentially cut off any hopes of extending this chase. The running was done. Coming to a complete stop at the car, Dominic slowed down and began catching his breath. Cross wanted to make sure there was nothing he was missing. Dominic Cross had already made the mistake of underestimating Jason Matthews once. It could be fatal if he made the same mistake a second time. Cross surveyed the vehicle and walking around the car, checking the trunk he saw Jason flee into. Jason Matthews was tightly sealed inside.

Treading carefully and looking around for those creatures, Dominic thought about burning the vehicle with Jason inside. Pulling the gas cap and stuffing the gas tank with clothes while lighting the clothes on fire. But Dominic didn't have access to matches or a lighter.

Walking to the driver's front side of the car, Dominic tried the door handle to the car and found the car door locked. Dominic pulled his elbow back and then, with force, launched his elbow forward, smashing the driver's side window. Pieces of glass shattered onto the ground outside the vehicle and into shards on the driver's seat inside.

Dominic then opened the car door and immediately cursed at himself. He had forgotten about the car alarm. The car alarm started blaring in the quiet of the night, filling the empty void of the night with unnecessary repeating beeping noises. The horn beeped, the headlights and warning lights blinked, and the alarm rhythmically kept sounding. The alarm was loud and would draw unwanted attention from those creatures, but what was done was done. Time to get on with what he needed to do. Dominic opened the car door and looked under the wheel dash finding the vehicle trunk latch. Dominic flipped the switch, and the trunk popped open.

Dominic took his knife out of his belt. Placing the edge of the blade on the side of the car, Cross scratched the side of the vehicle producing a screeching noise beneath the sound of the repetitive car alarm. Reaching the back of the trunk, Dominic decided to end the pursuit. Opening the vehicle's trunk, he saw, lying on his side curled in a fetal position Jason Matthews staring up at him.

Dominic smiled and watched as Jason raised his right arm and pointed an orange object up to him. Dominic did not get a clear view of the orange object and didn't have time to process what happened next until it was too late. The trunk illuminated red and smoky. Dominic Cross' cheek was smacked with a high-velocity projectile object just under his eye.

The impact of the high-velocity object on Dominic Cross's cheek broke the bone under his skin. The left side of Cross' face swelled up red as he staggered back several steps withering in pain. The swelling underneath the cheek so close to his eye caused temporary blindness rendering him unable to see. If the object had struck a few centimeters up, he could have been blinded for life. A god damn flare gun, he thought as the flare danced around, smoking red on the ground.

The pain was excruciating. His unaffected eye began to tear up as the pain on the other side of his face from the broken cheekbone set in. Through the tears, the smoke, and the pain, Cross tried to pull himself together as he danced around, staggering in pain. Still holding onto the knife, he tried to recollect himself to start a second attack on Jason Matthews. Looking back at the trunk, Dominic turned just in time to see Jason Matthews run up to him and strike him in the center of the face above his nose with a tire iron.

The tire iron blow knocked Dominic off his feet and put him on his back, knocking the wind out of his chest as he struck the ground. His face was battered, and blood poured from both of his nostrils. Jason, not wasting any time, continued the assault as Dominic lay on the ground defenseless. Striking Dominic four times about the chest and stomach with the tire iron. As Dominic covered his face with his arms, Jason continued striking at Cross' exposed chest area. Dominic could hear his ribs cracking as the blows from

155

the tire iron landed. Cross moaned in pain, and then the assault stopped as he felt something else, opening his eye and looking down. Cross saw Jason feeling the outside of his jean pockets. On the right side of Dominic's pocket, Jason found what he was looking for and, reaching into Dominic Cross' jean pocket, pulled out Dominic's car keys.

As Jason started to pull away with the car keys from Cross' jean pockets, Cross caught Jason's throat with his left hand and squeezed. Taking his right hand, Cross had recovered the knife he dropped when he was smacked in the face with the tire iron. Cross brought the knife up and swiped the knife at Jason's face. The blade caught Jason's forehead as he tried to pull away. Blood from the superficial wound poured into Jason's face. Trying to keep his space, Jason backed away and landed on his butt in front of Dominic.

Dominic, beaten and bloodied, sat up, rolled onto his side, and got one knee up in front of the other Cross attempting to stand up. Cross's balance and vision were both skewed. Despite being off-balance, Dominic's only intent was on harming Jason Matthews. Jason sat on the ground, looking up and staring at Dominic Cross as the injured man stood in front of him with the knife in hand. Then Jason did something out of the ordinary and curled up into a fetal position on the ground. Dominic's instinct took over, telling him something was wrong when Jason assumed this position.

With a mouth and nose full of blood and being blind in one eye, Dominic turned his head to look behind him. Cross could see car alarm lights and hear the vehicle making noise, and through the red glow of the flare smoking on the ground Cross saw movement. Moving quickly toward him was an albino creature. There was no time for an injured Dominic Cross to meet this threat as the attacker engaged him by jumping on Cross' back as he was starting to turn around to get ahead of the assault. Cross staggered to his side but was able to stay on his feet. The creature jumped upon Cross' back. Cross yelped in pain as the small albino dug its claws into the deltoids on both shoulders of Cross and then took a bite of Dominic's posterior shoulder muscle.

Cross took the knife in his right hand and implanted the blade into the creature's eye. The albino spasmed, releasing his grip on Dominic before falling limp to the ground dead. Cross shuddered in pain, but like a prizefighter, he was still on his feet.

Cross staggered on with blood running over the upper extremity of his torso from his head to his jeans. Jason, not wasting any time, got to his feet and pulled the tire iron before him, squaring up to face Dominic, who removed the knife from the deceased creature.

The two stared intensely at one another. Dominic was too tired to make the first move, and Jason was waiting to act in self-defense. A second creature attacking from Dominic Cross' blind side jumped up onto Dominic. This time the albino beast was able to take Cross off his feet. Both the albino attacker and Dominic Cross landed on the ground with a thud. The creature was able to get up first and position itself on top of an injured Dominic. Jason watched for only a few seconds as the two wrestled with one another on the ground; as the creature gained position on top of Dominic, Jason turned to leave before watching the albino beast devour Dominic Cross.

Pulling the key fob from his packet Jason Matthews turned the car alarm off. Backing away from the body of Dominic Cross with the creature still on top of him, Jason made his way to the vehicle Cross arrived in. Opening the door, Jason placed the key in the starter and turned the car engine on. Placing the headlights on Jason Matthews began driving towards route seventy-two to get help for his friends in the tunnels below if they were still alive.

30 - Marcus Robertson

Brooke Mueller held a broken flashlight leading the group through the tunnel while Marcus assisted Abrams following from the rear. Traveling what seemed to be several hundreds of yards, Abrams held his injured right hand, which flopped back and forth at the wrist as he moved in his left hand above his head to slow down the bleeding. Despite keeping Abrams on his feet, the group had to take frequent breaks to let Abrams rest. Abrams requested to sit down several times, but Marcus and Brooke did their best to keep him on his feet, fearing if he sat down, Abrams might not ever get back up.

Marcus was no longer holding the vest to the side of his face as the blood was still draining from his missing ear. Up ahead was another cavern that intersected between the tunnel they were in and three other tunnel openings in front of them. This cavern was altogether different from any they had seen to this point. The cavern was large and oval and had a circular shape with structure going around. But most importantly, the ceiling above had caved in. A large ten-foot opening in the roof of the grotto leading to the outside could be observed.

Through the ceiling, the three of them could see the moon, stars, and passing clouds in the sky as they stood on the floor of the cave staring at the night sky. The ledge from the top of the ceiling, where they would need to reach to exit the tunnel system, was about six or seven feet up from where they were standing. None of them was tall enough to reach the top and leave the cavern on their own.

"I have an idea. I can lift Brooke up to the top. When she is up there, she can reach down, and while I support Abrams on my back and push him up while Brooke pulls him up. Then I can run and jump, and you two can catch me and pull me up." Marcus said.

Abrams was silent, knowing he was the least useful in this situation and, at best, was a detriment to the group because of his hand injury. Brooke, however, stared at Marcus and then his belly and then up at the opening in the ceiling exit.

"You will never be able to jump up there, and I will never be able to pull you up either. I don't have the upper body strength." Brooke said.

Marcus placed his hands on his portly stomach frame as if disagreeing.

"I have a better idea. I'll crouch down and let you step on my back like a stool. You reach up, and when you start pulling yourself up, Abrams and I can push on the heels of your feet to boost you up. Once you get up, we can repeat with Abrams going next. He'll need your help getting up. After, I can run and grab your dangling arms, and you two can pull me up." Brooke said.

Brooke positioned herself underneath the ledge of the opening without waiting for a consensus and crouched down on all fours. Marcus didn't like the plan but obliged, not wanting to waste any more time in the tunnels with an avenue of escape so close above them.

Marcus stepped on Brooke's back and reached for the top of the ledge, trying to hold on and pull himself up. Beneath him, Brooke started to stand up, pushing with her back against Marcus' feet. Finding a firm grip on the edge of the opening, Marcus began to get some air pulling himself up. Below him, Abrams pushed on the bottom of Marcus' heel with his left hand, and Brooke was driving on the bottom of Marcus' other heel with both hands.

Struggling, Marcus finally got his belly over the ledge and out of the tunnel system in the nighttime air above. He gasped for air, not realizing how hard it was for him to do an actual pull-up, even with the assistance of two people. Marcus rolled over onto his stomach and peered back down in the hole. Below him, Marcus could see Abrams holding his hand, and Brooke stood waiting for him. Both were looking up at him.

"I'm good." Marcus yelled down to them and motioning with his hand for the next person to begin their ascent.

Again, Brooke Mueller crouched down beneath the same ledge opening in the ceiling, and Abrams stepped on her back. The first time positioning himself on Brooke's back, Abrams lost his balance and fell off. The second time, after gaining some height and with Brooke's assistance, he grabbed hold of Marcus' outstretched hand. But the two of them were sweaty and lost grip with one another, resulting in Abrams falling down on his back again.

Abrams and Marcus were then wiping their hands off on their clothes, preparing for a third attempt. Brooke crouched down, and with Abrams stepping on her back, reached up for Marcus' outstretched hands. Taking his one good left arm in both of his arms, Marcus pulled with everything he possessed. Beneath Abrams, Brooke pushed on the bottom of both of Abrams' shoes. Abrams, covered in sweat, made his best attempt at a one arm left-handed pull-up.

Marcus getting Abrams halfway to the top, reached over the back of Abrams to the back of his jeans, and grabbing hold of Abrams belt, began to pull Abrams up by the literal seat of his pants. Fully expending all of his energy, Marcus rolled Abrams over on top of his own body and to safety.

The two men gasped for air, and Marcus began rubbing his hands in the dirt to clear the sweat so when he grabbed for Brooke, there would be no slippage. Hanging over the ledge and again peering into the cave tunnel intersection, Marcus let both of his arms hang down as low as they could go outstretched. To his surprise, Abrams laid down next to him, ready to assist using his one good left arm.

Brooke stepped back to the farthest wall and, taking three deep breathes, ran up the dirt in the middle of the cave. Reaching the top portion of the mound from the cave-in on the floor in the center of the cave, Brooke jumped and, with her fingers, just managed to grab hold of Marcus's hands. He had her, Marcus thought, holding onto Brooke with both hands. Abrams lying down next to Marcus, started to reach for Brooke with his left hand and assist Marcus in pulling Brooke up.

Then there was a sharp tug on her body. Marcus and Abrams both lost their grip on Brooke's hands. As if in a slow downward motion, Brooke fell seven feet back down into the shaft and tunnel system below. When Brooke landed, she almost bounced off the ground below. Marcus could see Brooke expel the air from her lungs through her lips in the cavern below in the moonlight.

Below Marcus saw the albino figure which had caused Brooke to fall. Tangled underneath Brooke from the fall, the creature had jumped on Brooke, bringing her back down to the ground below. The albino creature recovering faster than Brooke was now grabbing her leg as she kicked and fought, as the figure was attempting to pull her into the tunnel. A second creature from an opposite direction attacked Brooke's vulnerable side.

Marcus could see Brooke below kicking, screaming, fighting both creatures. Using her arms and feet to try and fend off her attackers as they ripped at her. Marcus got into a crouching position and got ready to do the heroic thing and jump down and save Brooke. However, Abrams placed his body weight on top of Marcus's, pinning him with his good left arm. Unwilling to release Marcus into the pit below.

"Don't jump. She's already gone." Abrams said, clutching at Marcus's shirt and shoulder with his left hand.

Looking down below over the ledge, Marcus could see Brooke being dragged into a tunnel beneath them out of sight by the two creatures. Her screams were already fading into silence. Marcus had wanted to jump down there and rescue Brooke. Seeing Brooke dragged away and murdered by the two creatures would forever be a moment Marcus would see every night in his dreams for the rest of his life. Knowing someone who saved him died while Marcus had to sit idly by, powerless to prevent their death.

Taking a deep breath from the anxiety of seeing the murder of Brooke below, the two men laid on their backs and stared at the night sky.

"There was nothing either of us could do." Abrams repeatedly said, maybe to reassure himself more than Marcus.

Resting for a moment, Marcus was the first to get up onto his feet. Once up, Marcus was able to help Abrams get to his feet. Looking around in the dark, the two men tried to determine where they were. There was no grass, and the reeds around them were brown and dead. When the wind blew, dirt flowed in their direction. Both men now realized where they were, about twenty or twenty-five yards from the dirt road going into Walnford Plantation.

The pair walked towards the dirt stone road and then, upon finding the road, started to walk toward route seventy-two. Route seventy-two was miles from where they currently were, but the only other option was heading back towards Walnford Plantation, which didn't seem too appealing. The pair were outside, away from the danger in the tunnels below. Abrams was holding his right hand in the air, and Marcus was walking next to him.

Behind them, the two men heard a car kicking up stones coming from the direction of Walnford Plantation. The headlights were approaching them. There was nowhere to run, no place to hide. This was the time to stand their ground and fight.

"When the car stops, and if they get out of the car, rush at them. The men shooting at us weren't very good shots, to begin with, and at this close range, we can try and seize the opportunity and use the rush opportunity to our advantage. Otherwise, we are sitting ducks. Whoever is in the car may be able to shoot at us, but he won't get both of us." Abrams said.

"I'd rather go down fighting right now. I'm too tired and angry to run anymore." Marcus said.

The two men stopped on the side of the dirt road and watched as the headlights moving towards them grew brighter. The car stopped about ten feet from them, and the driver's side door opened up, and a familiar voice could be heard.

"Do you gentlemen need a ride?" Jason Matthews said, coming around to the front of the vehicle. Jason was entirely covered in feces. Blood flowed from a gash on his forehead. Jason Matthews and Marcus quickly embraced before helping Abrams get into the center of the car's front seat. Marcus sat in the passenger seat, and Jason resumed driving.

The three men were silent, driving past Speedy's restaurant towards route seventy-two. Jason was driving them following signs posted along route seventy-two for a hospital.

"What happened to the girl you were with?" Jason asked.

"She didn't make it. She saved our lives, and we couldn't save her." Marcus said with tears in his eyes.

There was no further exchange of words spoken during the rest of the car ride to the hospital. The three men were beaten and bloodied. No further conversation about what they endured that evening needed to be had.

31 - Dominic Cross

Erroneous reports of Dominic Cross's demise were greatly exaggerated. Fifteen minutes had passed with Dominic laying on the ground before Cross reopened his eye. His other eye swelled shut from the flare gun attack. Dominic Cross flashbacked to events that had occurred before he passed out. He was holding the knife, and Jason Matthews possessed the tire iron. The two men were squaring up to fight one another when a creature was drawn to the vicinity by the repetitive noise of the car alarm. This was the second creature to save Jason Matthew's life in less than a minute.

The first creature had been knifed in the eye by Dominic Cross, but it was the second creature's attack that took Cross off his feet. The albino creature was fresh to the fight, whereas Cross was slowed by the beating he had taken to this point. The albino attacker got on top of Cross and was about to start the process of cannibalizing its prey.

As Jason Matthews started backing away from the creature believing the fight was over. Cross plunged the knife into the creature's stomach and filleted the fucker from the stomach to the creature's lungs while the dying creature bled out on top of him. Blood flowed from the creature's stomach, and in the darkness, the rush of blood-covered Dominic Cross as he lay below underneath the dying cannibal. Cross held his forearm underneath the creature's chin preventing the creature from biting at him. On top, the creature spasmed, shivered, and shuddered as he expired. From Jason Matthews's inattentive perspective, he interpreted the movements as the creature eating away at Dominic, with all the blood pouring out on top of Dominic. Fatigued beyond measure after killing the beast on top of him, Cross passed out.

Exhausted from the events of the night, Cross awoke underneath the dead body on top of him. The car alarm was turned off. Quiet had returned to the peace of the night. Pushing the creature off of him, Cross was covered in shit and blood as he rolled over and placed the knife back into his belt. Getting up was a challenge as his ribs were badly bruised from the assault by Jason Matthews with the tire iron.

As he stood up, Cross looked with his one good eye in the distance at the building outlines in the dark as the moon cast a yellow glow overhead. Dominic paid particular attention staring at the shape of the roof of the main building of Walnford Plantation, the building where he had gone into the basement and come up through a hole in the ground in the nearby trees. Cross imagined the building held a nefarious power in the moonlight as if something sinister had happened there a long time ago. Cross heard of such houses having influence over evil.

Not wanting to stick around to see any more of the creatures and with no more use for Walnford Plantation, Dominic Cross turned and started walking down the stone dirt road one foot at a time. Back toward civilization. As he stumbled ahead, looking to the east, the sky was a flame of pink met the shade of blackness from the night. The moon was no longer shaded with cloud cover, and the moon's glow was fading from view. Dawn was approaching, and a new day was coming.

Holding his ribs as he walked and taking each breath with mild pain in either his face, shoulder, chest, or torso, Cross put one slow step in front of the other. He would walk the dirt road back to route seventy-two if needed. Cross guessed the walk back would be about ten miles back to route seventy-two, maybe seven miles if he could find help at Speedy's restaurant, the restaurant they had passed on their way in the day before. Estimating an average mile would take Cross about sixteen minutes to walk. Walking injured could take Cross about twenty or twenty-two minutes to walk one mile. Maybe three hours of walking to route seventy-two, Cross thought as he stared ahead.

If anyone had seen Dominic Cross, covered in shit and blood. His left eye was swollen to the size of an apple, black and bruised. His nose busted from the tire iron, and his nasal and sinus passages filled with dried blood. His left shoulder missing a chunk of flesh, having been bitten away. Cross thought he should be the living embodiment of what Frankenstein's monster should look like following the resurrection.

The darkness of night was finally gone. The sun was still edging up on the horizon but was not yet wholly in the sky. In the distance of the dirt road, he saw Speedy's restaurant. Cross began hobbling toward the restaurant a little faster, reinvigorated about the prospect of getting some help. When he got to the porch where the door was, Cross banged on the restaurant's door repeatedly, but there was no answer. Peering in the windows, Cross did not see any movement.

Cross took two steps back and kicked the door open, breaking the lock on the door. With the front door slamming open, Cross stumbled inside and took a quick look around. He spotted a refrigerator behind the counter and hobbled over, opening the fridge and peering inside. Reaching his hand inside the top freezer, Cross pulled out a bag of frozen French fries.

With the frozen bag of French fries in hand, Cross hobbled back to the door he had kicked open and, after shutting the door closed, laid down at the base of the door on the floor. Cross placed the frozen bag of French fries on his face over his nose and eye, trying to bring down the swelling. His back against the door, Cross inhaled and exhaled as best he could through his mouth, the taste of blood was still in the back of his throat. After a few breath's Cross was asleep with exhaustion.

After lying on the floor for several hours, Dominic was awakened by the sounds of sirens and cars traveling past the restaurant down the dirt road towards Walnford Plantation. Cross got to his feet, his body hurting worse after the rest than before he laid down. Peeking out the restaurant window, he saw four State Trooper cars driving by with their lights flashing. Cross thought the cop cars would pull into the restaurant for a brief second and find him there.

But as they kept driving down the dirt road towards the plantation, this thought disappeared from consideration. Cross then looked in the corner of the store with his eye-catching hold of something he had not seen before in the dark. Laying on the floor was a dead creature. The dead creature's body was limp, and blood covered the back wall. The albino cannibal had been shot in the chest with a shotgun. Dominic walked up over to the body, and there was a giant hole in the cavity of the creature's chest. In front of the dead body was a hole in the wooden floor. The crater was similar to the one Cross crawled out of in the woods.

165

The creatures had dug tunnels seven miles out from under Walnford, Dominic said to himself. His thoughts changed when he saw the shotgun lying on the floor beside the hole. Cross reached down in pain and picked the shotgun up, racking the slide. An empty plastic shell casing ejected from the port, and a new round was racked in the chamber. Cross then spit a blood-filled luger down the black hole.

Turning around and walking away from the hole, Cross walked down the candy aisle picking up a Snickers bar from the rack. Holding the shotgun in one hand, Cross tore open the wrapper of the Snickers bar open with his teeth and took a bite of the chocolate candy bar as he walked towards the door behind the counter. Arriving at the door, Cross could hear scratch marks clawing at the closed door.

Cross pushed the rest of the Snickers bar into his mouth. Dominic began to chew on the candy bar, but the broken bones in his face discouraged his chewing, and he instead elected to let it melt inside his mouth before swallowing the rest whole. Reaching with his left hand while keeping the shotgun leveled at the door, Cross turned the doorknob and pushed the door forward with the shotgun barrel.

Before him, scratching at the door was an old grey dog wearing a red collar. Cross bent down as far as his ribs would allow him and pet the dog. The dog reciprocated, wagging his tail, and began licking the shit-covered hand of Dominic Cross. Cross then completed a quick sweep of the room the dog was locked in and saw a bathroom on his left. Entering the bathroom, Cross turned the lights on over the sink, and for a brief second, Cross didn't recognize the person staring back at him in the mirror. The bruises and swelling enlarged one side of his face, and his nose was distorted.

Placing the shotgun down next to the toilet, Cross began to remove his clothing. His shirt, underwear, and pants stained with shit and dried blood were stuck to his body, and given the injuries, he sustained Cross took longer than usual to pull the clothes off of himself. Completely naked, Cross set the shower dial at a high temperature and let the waterfall onto his muscular body.

Cross thought this was the best shower he had taken in his life. The steam filled the bathroom, and Cross using the bar of soap, started peeling away the dried blood sticking to his body and the clumps of feces stuck in his goatee and matted throughout his hair. The shower took longer than Cross expected to get clean, although truthfully, he did not mind the longer shower and the time to think.

Coming out of the shower dripping wet, Cross took the towel hanging on the towel rack and dried off. He went to the dresser and put Speedy's underwear and clothes on. Trying on the clothes was a tight fit. Cross looked in the mirror at the ill-fitted clothing guessing Speedy was a lot smaller and thinner than he was. But having no choice, he put the tight-fitting clothes on and ran his hand through his thick black hair. Seeing a ball cap hanging from the mirror, Cross grabbed the hat and placed the hat on his head to keep the injuries to his face concealed from anyone casually glancing past him.

Cross was walking better following the shower, the hobble in his gait had lessened, and his ribs, although still in pain, were not as severely injured as he initially suspected. Cross went back and picked up the shotgun from the bathroom. The dog lying on the bed watched Cross as he moved around his former master's room. Cross saw a medicinal aisle in the general store and started walking that way but stopped at the cash register, pushing a register button and watching the drawer pop open. Cross took the money in the register and checked underneath the cash tray where the larger bills were usually kept.

Under the tray, Cross found two hundred dollars in twenty-dollar bills. Cross took the cash and placed money in his pocket. Continuing to the medicine aisle, Cross put cortisone, Advil, and other disinfection ointments into his pants pockets. When Cross had finished grabbing the medical items and putting them in his pockets, he opened the Advil and took four tablets into his hand, swallowing them with no water. He then went into the back of the refrigerator and took two bottles of water.

Passing his way out the back door, shotgun in hand, bottles of pills in his pocket, Cross found the keys to the old white Ford pickup truck hanging from a hook on the wall. Cross picked the keys up, opened the back door, turned around, and looked at the dog.

"Come on. Do you want to ride with me?" Cross said to the dog.

Duke, the old grey dog with big brown eyes, wagged his tail and ran out the back door to the white truck. Cross opened the truck door, and Duke jumped in as Cross followed the dog inside the truck's cab sitting behind the steering wheel. The truck's ignition started on the first turn, and Cross rolled both windows down, allowing in a warm breeze of fresh air.

Cross drove the truck the three miles to route seventy-two, and when he reached the highway, he asked himself where he should go now. Mexico is always nice for a man with limited funds, he thought. Cross also had done time with the head of the Nomads chapter based out of Florida. He would be welcome there. Maybe, he should lay low for the winter. Get a cabin in Vermont and heal up and work out until the spring. Cross pet the dog behind the ears, and Duke had his tongue out, enjoying the fall weather.

With so many possibilities, so many adventures to choose from, living each day as they came, Dominic Cross decided on the simpler choice. He turned the steering wheel column and drove off to the right, not thinking about or planning anything in advance.

32 - Jason Matthews

Forty minutes after getting to route seventy-two, Jason Matthews drove Marcus and Abrams to the emergency room at Saint Mary's Community Hospital. Pulling up outside the emergency room door, the three men exited the car, with Marcus and Jason escorting and holding Abrams up as they moved. The waiting room was empty at this time in the morning. The nurse on duty looked up at the three of them moving to the emergency room registration desk. The three men who entered before her were covered in blood and shit. One man had his hand dangling with a tourniquet at the wrist.

"We need help." Jason said to her.

The nurse paged for staff assistance, emergency assistance in the waiting room area and hit the emergency call button located on her desk. Two female nurses entered the waiting room and, seeing Abrams, helped him onto a gurney. While Jason and Marcus stood there, Abrams was taken into the back room as the automatic double doors closed behind them.

A third nurse came out, a male nurse, and seeing Jason and Marcus had the pair of men seated in wheelchairs. The male nurse then took Marcus behind the double doors and into a separate emergency room in the opposite direction Abrams had departed.

Leaving only Jason in the emergency room waiting area sitting in a wheelchair with a cut on his forehead. A fourth nurse came out and, holding her nose in her hand, wheeled Jason into the exam room. In the exam room, the nurse gagged before asking Jason his name, address, insurance information, and after taking his vitals, what the purpose of Jason's visit was today.

"My wife tried to have me killed, and her hitmen chased me through an underground cavern of shit where some monsters attacked us and tried to eat me."

The nurse's face indicated she didn't know what to think, but Jason Matthews asked the nurse repeatedly to call the police and have them respond to Walnford Plantation outside of Tunica as other lives may be in jeopardy. The nurse left the room, leaving Jason Matthews sitting in the wheelchair. He could overhear a few words the nurse speaking with her supervisor said. Paranoid. Traumatic events. Possible drug or psychological issues.

Jason Matthews didn't argue when the nurse came back. Having someone not believe your story about flesh-eating cannibals was another thing, and his story would be invalidated if he acted argumentative in the hospital. A second nurse came in after the first nurse. This nurse wanted to know about Jason's friends and any information he could provide as both were being prepared for surgery.

"Any information you could provide on the two gentlemen you arrived with would be helpful." The nurse said.

"The shorter man with the missing ear, his name is Marcus Robertson, he works at Georgia University with myself and most likely carries the same insurance plan as I have." Jason paused while the nurse wrote the information down.

"The second man, his name is Abrams." Jason said.

"Abrams? is that a first or last name?" The nurse asked.

"It's just Abrams. We just met him tonight. He may be a private detective." Jason replied.

"We are going to ask that you spend the night here just to be on the safe side." The nurse placed an IV fluid and heart monitor on Jason. The nurse also asked Jason to remain in the wheelchair as she wheeled him to an elevator and hit a high number button on the elevator. When the elevator dinged and opened, Jason was wheeled to a room. The nurse placed out two pairs of gowns and left a trash bag for his clothing.

"You can get out of the clothes you are wearing and shower. There are soap packages located on the sink in the container, as well as a toothbrush. After your shower, please place your gown on. The opening goes in back. You may place your soiled clothing in the trash bag. Please remove any valuables before placing articles in the trash bag." The nurse said before exiting the room.

Taking a shower with an IV fluid in his arm was uncomfortable as the IV cord kept rubbing against Jason's face and getting crossed up in his arms. The small packets of soap were not enough to remove the clumps of blood and matted feces from his hair, fingernails, and body. Lumps of shit kept having to be scrubbed out, with pieces of feces hidden in Jason's ears and belly button.

Getting out of the shower, Jason got dressed in the hospital gown, opening the back as requested. The dressing gown opened to the back revealed his ass. Sticking his head out the hospital corridor, Jason saw the nurse on duty and asked her if the police had been contacted. The nurse told him she had passed the information and the request on to her supervisor. Going back to his room, Jason sat on the bed, and a different nurse brought a small plastic cup of pills.

"What are these?" Jason asked.

"A sedative to help you relax, and pain medication. Both low doses." The nurse said.

Jason took the medications and chased them down with a small drink of water. Laying under the covers, Jason closed his eyes and, before he could count to ten, was asleep.

When Jason opened his eyes, he saw he had a roommate, a man he recognized as Marcus Robertson. Marcus lay in a bed next to Jason only instead of sleeping, Marcus was watching television. The blinds on the windows were open and, based on the amount of light, it appeared to be mid-day as the sun was shining brightly into the white hospital room.

"Good morning, or should I say good afternoon." Marcus said, turning his head to look at Jason. The bandage wrapped around Marcus's head and missing ear were visible, and Jason grimaced, looking at the bandages, remembering how they looked after the ear had first been eaten off.

"I was in surgery for over two hours." Marcus said.

"Luckily, Mississippi has an excellent ear transplant specialist unit or, so I was told. Nothing science can't fix now. I can choose a removable plastic ear, complete with an earpiece, or I can choose to grow an ear on a pig and have the pig ear transplanted onto my head. The wonders of science? Of course, we have a shitty HMO plan, so good luck getting pre-approval for a pig's ear." Marcus said with a smile.

"How are you otherwise?" Jason asked, sitting up in the bed.

"I'm a little fucked up. I didn't expect to make it out of that tunnel system alive. Brooke saved my life, and in return, I couldn't do anything to save her." Marcus said.

A nurse wheeled a third patient sleeping in a bed into the room. The patient was Abrams. The male nurse who wheeled the bed into the room and set up the monitors said Abrams would be asleep for a while but that his overall diagnosis was good. Marcus and Jason both saw but did not say the obvious, Abrams was missing his right hand. A dressing sleeve was pulled up over the missing appendage.

With Abrams now in the room, Marcus and Jason both became quiet. There was nothing further to discuss or joke around about. Instead, they sat and watched Doctor Phil on television. An hour later, just before two in the afternoon, a police officer showed up. The officer was Sheriff Reilly, the same Sheriff running for re-election and who Abrams had met with in his office three days ago.

"What the hell you boys doing up by Walnford Plantation?" Reilly asked both Jason and Marcus as he took out a notepad to take their statements.

"We were writing a book about pre-civil war plantations and slavery; we are professors from Georgia State University." Marcus said, lying.

"And what exactly happened to you boys?" Reilly asked, putting the pen in the corner of his mouth.

"My wife tried to have us killed. She hired three people to kill us." Jason said.

"Why would your wife do that?" Sheriff Reilly asked.

"My life insurance through the University where I work, the life insurance is valued at over five hundred thousand dollars. If I died, the money would all go to her." Jason said.

"How did this private detective, Abrams, how did he fit in all this?" Sheriff Reilly asked, pointing his pen in Abrams' direction.

"He saved our lives." Jason said to the Sheriff.

"When they took us hostage, Abrams and Brooke freed us, and running from the killers, we ran into the main building house at Walnford and then into the basement." Jason said.

"Where is your wife now, Mr. Matthews?" Sheriff Reilly asked.

"She's most likely dead. When we ran into the basement, we slipped into a cave system through a crack in the basement

172

foundation and wall. While we were attempting to escape, we were attacked by cannibals." Jason said.

"And you saw your wife get killed by these cannibals?" Sheriff Reilly asked, unconvinced.

"No. No, I didn't see my wife killed; she could be alive in the tunnel system under the plantation. But I would think it's hardly likely." Jason said.

"What about this female companion for Mr. Abrams? Brooke? Where is she?" Sheriff Reilly asked.

"She's dead." Marcus said.

"You saw this?" Sheriff Reilly asked.

"Yes. Brooke died saving the lives of Abrams and me." Marcus said.

"How exactly did she die, Mr. Robertson?" Sheriff Reilly asked.

"Two of those cannibals ripped her to shreds, and dragged her body into the tunnels, and ate her." Marcus said, tearing up.

"What about these hired killers? What happened to them?" Sheriff Reilly asked.

"The creatures got at least two of them. I can't say for sure what happened to the third man." Jason said, lying to protect Abrams, who shot killed the female who took them hostage.

"Cannibalistic Creatures? That's the story we are sticking with?" Sheriff Reilly asked both of them.

"You should get the national guard out there, quarantine the area. If anyone did survive any search parties going in, there would be in grave danger." Jason said.

"I just want to make sure I have this correct. Both of your stories are that while traveling for research on a book, your wife hired three killers to bump you off for the insurance money. Mr. Abrams and his companion came along coincidently, and the four of you escape into the basement. Escaping and fighting off-contract killers and cannibalistic creatures. That's your story?" Sheriff Reilly asked.

"The stories all true." A voice from the right side of the room said. The three men looked over, and their gaze was returned by Abrams looking at them being interviewed by the Sheriff.

"What they are telling you is true, Sheriff. I would not have believed their story myself if I had not been there." Abrams said.

173

"So, if I send the State Police to Walnford Plantation, what are they going to find Mr. Abrams?" Sheriff Reilly asked him.

"I would advise anyone who goes there to be extremely careful." Abrams said, shutting his eyes and resting his head on the pillow.

Sheriff Reilly stepped outside the room, and with Abrams watching from his bed, he could see Sheriff Reilly make two telephone calls with his cellphone. The first call did not last very long, and the Sheriff was off the phone in a few seconds. The second call was significantly longer in duration. When Sheriff Reilly finished, he hung up the cell phone and walked back into the room.

"I just contacted the State Police. They are sending several officers, forensics, and a rescue team to Walnford Plantation. I have to go and meet them there. For the first time in thirty years, I needed to call the State Police for assistance, so you had better be telling the truth for your sake. I would ask you not to leave town if you are discharged without permission." Sheriff Reilly said, finishing his speech before leaving.

Jason came over to Abrams and said, "I wanted to give this back to you and say thank you for saving our lives." Jason placed Abrams' cell phone on the small table next to Abrams' hospital bed.

"I was able to buy a universal charger in the gift shop and power the phone for you last night." Jason said.

"Thank you." Abrams said, leaving the phone alone and looking at his missing hand. He began to cry. Later in the evening, Abrams took the cell phone in his left hand and began to scroll through his e-mail from the last two days. One of the e-mails was from his partner in response to the pictures of the vehicles located at Ace One Towing Company. Abrams read the e-mail twice and placed his head back down on the pillow, and went back to sleep from the medications he was on.

The following day, the doctor walked in and informed Jason he would be discharged in a few hours but that Marcus and Abrams would be there for observation and post-operation rest for a few days. A nurse following up let Jason know his clothing was laundered for him but that Abrams and Marcus would need new clothing as their clothing was cut up as they were prepared for surgery. When the nurse left, and the three of them were alone again, Marcus spoke.

"It's a shame we never found that gold." Marcus said.

"With all those tunnels and creatures under the house down there, maybe the gold will never be found. Maybe, the gold never existed at all." Marcus said.

"Oh, the gold exists. It just was never in the cave." Jason said.

"You can't know that for sure." Marcus said.

"I think I can, and I am pretty sure I know where the gold is hidden," Jason retorted.

Abrams, who had his eyes closed, opened them up with the revelation Jason knew where the gold was.

Jason and Marcus both walked over to the small table beside Abrams, who remained lying down. Jason produced the photocopy of the letter from Robert Hillman and the copy of the map his wife insisted he make. Papers he had removed from his pockets before having his clothing laundered.

"The only thing good thing Tammy did do was to tell us to photocopy this map." Jason said.

Opening the three pages up, Jason scrolled down the letter with his finger until he came upon the passage.

"We missed the clue, the location was obvious, and we overcomplicated matters and missed it. We got caught up in that basement, the photograph of the basement, the history of the basement, and we overlooked the obvious."" Jason repeated.

"What am I missing?" Marcus said.

"Hillman could not have known about the crack in the wall or the underground labyrinth of tunnels until after he hid the gold and turned himself over to the Walnford family for help." Jason said

"Additionally, look at these passages. In one sentence, Hillman says he is on a wagon injured, and he passes out. When he wakes up and sees a farm plantation. Now when he goes to them for help, he is on horseback. The wagon and gold are gone. But where did wagon go? Many trees circled the property, but he wouldn't leave a cart of gold in the open. Anyone could find it. Hillman also doesn't have the strength or time to dig and hide the gold because he is injured. You have been to the property, lots of dead grass, and a dirt road. Open space for miles around. So, where did Hillman stash the cart filled with gold?" Jason asked.

"The answer came to me after I hit my head and fell unconscious in the tunnels. As I was lying there, looking up at the

175

exit hole from the tunnel system. I didn't have time to think about the gold before then, but the answer just came to me as I lay there. Hillman took the cart and placed the wagon in the lake. He rode the wagon cart into the lake, and once the wagon was submerged, he cut the horses free. Taking one of the remaining horses, he went to the main house and asked for help." Jason said with a smile.

"The gold sank to the bottom of the lake. Look at the map. The answer is obvious. The lake is in the center of the drawing. The houses, fields, and farms, none of them are in the center. Hillman deliberately put the lake in the center. At the center of the map was our X marks the spot. We've all been there, nothing but empty space, empty yards, dead grass, dirt roads, only the houses and the lake, nothing else for miles around." Jason said.

Following Jason's revelation about the location of the gold being stashed in the lake, Marcus laid back down in his bed, and Jason took his laundered clothes out of the bag and started to get dressed.

"I'll get you, gentlemen, some clothes when I return to see you both later tonight." Jason said.

"Jason, don't take this the wrong way, but I'm not going back there, not for the gold, not ever." Marcus said.

"I don't think you could pay me enough to go back there and look for the gold Marcus." Jason said patting his friends' foot with his hand.

As Jason got dressed, the three men were silent, and although there was no further discussion on the matter, they all had the same thought. Gold was at the bottom of Walnford Plantation Lake.

33 - Beau Cameron

Thirty-two hours after Jason, Marcus, Abrams, and Brooke went into the crack in the wall, Beau Cameron was sitting in his tow truck. The owner of Advanced One towing received a call from Sheriff Reilly.

"Another abandoned car, Sheriff?" Beau said answering the cell phone dispensing with the needs to be formal.

"Beau, I need you to listen now son, I'm over here past Speedy's restaurant, and the shit has definitely hit the fan. I'm talking national guard level. There are two cars which I want picked up discreetly. Can you come and grab them?" Sheriff Reilly asked.

"Of course, Sheriff, I'll be right over." Beau said and hanging up the phone.

Beau turned on the road for Speedy's restaurant, taking the twenty-minute drive through town and east on route seventy-two while taking the time to stop for coffee. Driving up to the restaurant was a checkpoint with wooden barricades and six men in fatigues carrying M-16 assault rifles. Trying to make the turn off of route seventy-two Beau was hassled by men at the checkpoint. After a brief argument, Beau was allowed to proceed with an escort towards Walnford Plantation.

Arriving at the plantation's main house, Beau saw no less than four mobile trailer offices were placed in a circle formation, and several military Humvees were parked outside. Men in military and State Police uniforms jostled from position to position. On the perimeter of the main Walnford house, some men were setting up electric lights preparing for the dark.

The military men escorting Beau instructed him to hurry up and stop looking around. After fifteen minutes of hooking the first of two cars up to his tow truck, Sheriff Reilly came out of one of the mobile command trailers and was visibly upset talking to himself.

"Hello, Sheriff." Beau said as the Sheriff walked by him.

"Fuck these motherfuckers. Too many God Damn chiefs and not enough fucking Indians. I'm leaving. They can call me if they need to." Sheriff Reilly said, walking away and getting into his squad car. The Sheriff slammed the door to his vehicle and drove away, kicking up a bunch of dust.

Driving the first car back to his shop and unhooking the car, Beau grabbed another coffee at the local convenience store as he started back to Walnford for the second car. This time-traveling east on seventy-two took two hours as traffic was backed up near the checkpoint. The checkpoint he encountered previously had moved up to the road to where the initial turn-off for Speed's restaurant was located. Several State Police cars were operating the checkpoint, and after speaking with no less than four different officers, Beau was finally allowed to drive on to Walnford plantation. As Beau sat at the checkpoint, he could see and smell of smoke rising against the black of the night and a red bounce in the distance.

After waiting for an escort to arrive, Beau drove the three miles past the checkpoint turn-off, passing what used to be Speedy's restaurant. The restaurant was now a giant flame, as several military men surrounded the burning building holding their rifles at port arms. Beau couldn't help but notice some of the army-looking men were equipped with flame throwers. Driving the next seven miles to the main building of Walnford Plantation, Beau passed fifteen or twenty police, EMS, military, and government response vehicles.

Arriving to pick up the second vehicle in the dark of night, the military and government agencies had set up a perimeter of lights surrounding their makeshift compound with parked cars. Men in tactical gear stood looking out from their positions at the parked vehicles staring out into the darkness with night vision goggles.

Beau was again directed to hurry up and get the vehicle towed away. Beau was distracted to see men wearing hazmat suits entering and leaving the main Walnford house while he was working under the fluorescent lights. Other men were carrying flame thrower packs on their backs moved in unison towards the main house. Other men were wearing tin foil suits taking seismic readings of the ground, looking for something below the surface.

Beau would tell other customers, bar patrons, and townspeople about what he saw in the coming weeks. Not many people believed him as there was no news about anything other than five officers and two emergency rescue officers dying in a cave-in at Walnford Plantation during a rescue mission.

No less than two days after all of the commotion surrounding Walnford Plantation had occurred, all officers and military personnel were evacuated. The three houses which had stood for the last two hundred years had been taken apart and demolished by backhoes, excavators, and bulldozers. Several holes discovered on the grounds at Walnford Plantation had dynamite dropped into them by surveying crews, effectively destroying any tunnels or escape routes.

There was no evidence of any crimes. No persons or cannibals were discovered or reported, according to any official reports. No persons dead or alive were reported as recovered. It was as if Walnford Plantation was wiped from the face of Mississippi in three days.

34 – Abrams

Two months following the events at Walnford Plantation, Sheriff Reilly won re-election as Sheriff of Walnford county. After a weekend of celebrating by fishing, Sheriff Reilly returned to work on a Monday morning, ready to resume his work for the next three years. He was sitting at his desk filling out paperwork when the receptionist called and said two men were here to see him. When Reilly asked who was here, the receptionist said one word, a Mr. Abrams.

When Abrams and the unintroduced second man walked into Sheriff Reilly's office, Sheriff Reilly stood up and shook both of their hands. The Sheriff shook hands with Abrams using his left hand.

"Well, Mr. Abrams, I have to say, I didn't expect to see or hear from you again. What can I help you with?" Sheriff Reilly said, sitting down behind his desk and crossing his legs as he leaned back in his chair.

"Well, sir, I wanted to start by expressing my congratulations to you for winning your re-election Sheriff, nicely done. Also, thank you for taking the time to see me on such short notice." Abrams started.

"You see, I was at Advanced One towing about two months ago. While I was there with Brooke Mueller looking at her missing sister's car, I met with Beau, the owner, and took pictures of several license plates of some of the vehicles which were abandoned there by their owners. It wasn't until I was in the hospital on the day you visited coincidently, I was able to check my e-mail, and I received an unusual e-mail from my partner Allan Butler. Turns out all seven people who owned those vehicles, vehicle license plates I took pictures of, and whose cars are currently housed at Advanced One Towing were reported missing." Abrams said.

"Now, now, Mr. Abrams, this isn't going to be about monsters or cannibals, is it? I'm afraid that investigation didn't go so far and was found to have no basis." Sheriff Reilly said, laughing and attempting to demean Abrams in front of the unknown person Abrams had brought with him.

"As I was saying, I received an e-mail from my partner informing me all these missing people cars are being housed at Advanced One Towing. But this information conflicted with the information you gave me when I visited with you two months ago. You told me during our last conversation, there had only been four missing person cases in your district in the last thirty years." Abrams said.

"So, after going to physical therapy, and after getting myself well, I reached out to the Mississippi Attorney General's office and let them know I had information regarding at least seven people who had disappeared over the last three years. But in reality, this number could be far greater and could go back over several years." Abrams continued.

"Wouldn't you know, the Mississippi Attorney General thought enough of my claims to assign the man sitting next to me, Assistant United States Attorney for the great state of Mississippi, Mr. Joe Johnston, to look into this matter. So last week, without a search warrant, we went over to Advanced One Towing and spoke with the owner, Beau." Abrams said.

"The boy Beau doesn't have a brain in his head." Sheriff Reilly said.

"That may be Sheriff, but he apparently does have an excellent memory and an even better computer record of all the vehicles he has impounded. Letting Beau know his shop could be closed down and he could be sent to prison for conspiracy to tamper with evidence in several missing person cases, Beau was nice enough to let us look at the other twenty-two vehicles he had in his impound lot. Can you guess how many of those people are reported as missing?" Abrams asked.

Sheriff Reilly sat quiet, unimpressed.

"That's correct Sheriff, all twenty-two of those cars belong to current missing persons. When Beau was confronted with this information, he claimed this was the first he had heard of any missing persons. When the Assistant United States Attorney said Beau could be looking at conspiracy charges related to the covering up of crimes and the disappearance of people, would you know Beau asked for immunity and agreed to testify. Beau then proceeded to hand over the records of all the cars he impounded for the last seven years previous to the last three. Forty-six more cars he had sold at auction. We ran the information. All forty-six of those cars had their owners reported missing at some point in time. Seventy-five missing people in one jurisdiction Sheriff. All with one thing in common. Sheriff Reilly called the tow truck up, and Sheriff Reilly never bothered to follow up on any of these missing people." Abrams said.

"You have no evidence I called Beau to come and get those vehicles." Sheriff Reilly said.

"Do you want to know what else Beau at Advanced One Towing told us? He would bribe you one thousand dollars a year, so you would call him to tow these cars away." Abrams said.

"That was a Christmas gift." Sheriff Reilly said.

"The limit for a government official to accept from an individual he does business with is twenty dollars a year." Abrams said.

"Is this all you have? I accepted a thousand dollars, and there's a crime against having cars towed away? Please. If that's all, you gentlemen have come here to say. I could have saved you, gentlemen, a trip to my office." Sheriff Reilly said.

"No, but it is a dereliction of your duty as a sworn law enforcement officer and of your office not to report missing people or cars reported as missing. I guess if word got out that seventy-five people disappeared over ten years, there might be a hitch in your re-election campaign." Abrams said.

"But you are right Sheriff, what if there was gross incompetence on your part to not follow up on all those missing persons. There is still the bribery, and if you were willing to accept bribes from one person, why not another?" Abrams asked rhetorically.

"I don't have to listen to this. I'm going to ask you, gentlemen, to leave now. Anything further, you can speak to my attorney." Sheriff Reilly said, now standing up.

"Who did you call the day you visited me in the hospital, Sheriff? Who did you place a phone call to before calling in the State Police? I was watching you dial on your cell phone in the hospital in the hallway. Who did you call?" Abrams said, still seated.

"I won't listen to you besmirch my name or my title." Sheriff Reilly said, picking up the phone for the receptionist but having no one answer the receiver on the other end of the phone.

"I spoke with Speedy at the restaurant before he disappeared. He said there were regular trucks from Kingsford Chemical driving through a couple of times a week. Speedy thought the drivers were driving out to Walnford Plantation to sleep out there and passing through for a bite to eat. But I would bet they were dumping hazardous waste in that lake. I would bet Kingsford Chemical paid you to be their lookout and make sure things stayed quiet. After all, why else would they be driving to Walnford Plantation? Down a desolate road almost four counties away from their factory? I'll ask you again, Sheriff, who did you call first from the hospital that day before calling the State Police?" Abrams said, pressing Sheriff Reilly.

Sheriff Reilly didn't say anything, and Assistant United States Attorney Joe Johnston leaned over to Sheriff Reilly's desk and placed an envelope on the desk. The Sheriff picked the envelope up and started to read the contents of the paperwork.

"What is this?" Sheriff Reilly asked regarding the paperwork the Assistant United States Attorney placed on his desk.

"There is your copy of a search warrant for all of your bank records, phone bills, election accounts, office paperwork, and your household. Oh, and your safety deposit box." Abrams said, smiling.

"Did I tell you, Sheriff, Mr. Johnston's roommate in college is an IRS agent right here in the Mississippi area. After telling the local magistrate about the bribes by Beau, he signed our copy of that search warrant last week. There were several discrepancies in the election accounts and in your personal bank account the IRS would love to talk to you about, but most of all, the IRS would love to talk to you about the three-hundred and seventy-five thousand dollars in cash found in your safety deposit box." Abrams said.

"Go fuck yourself Mr. Abrams." Sheriff Reilly said, spitting across his desk onto Abrams.

"Who was it you called at the hospital that day before calling the State Police?" Abrams asked again.

"I am not answering your questions without an attorney." Sheriff Reilly said.

"It's okay, a search of your phone records already has informed us the call was placed to the vice president of operations at

Kingsford Chemical. Admit Kingsford Chemical was bribing you to dump toxic waste into the lake of Walnford Plantation, and this could go a lot easier on you." Abrams said.

"Fuck you Abrams. I'll see you in hell before I answer to you." Sheriff Reilly said.

Abrams and Johnston both got up, and as they opened the door to exit the office, a group of IRS agents with boxes entered the office and began seizing Sheriff Reilly's computer and paperwork. As several agents moved about the office, another IRS agent began mirandizing the Sheriff as another agent placed Sheriff Reilly in handcuffs after relieving the Sheriff of his firearm and belt.

35 - Jason Matthews

Eight months following the events at Walnford Plantation, Jason Matthews and Marcus Robertson's lives had returned to a steady form of routine. Jason had returned to work after only missing two weeks. Marcus went to work with only one ear for several months until a matching ear was transplanted from a pig. The pig match of an ear was not an exact match to Marcus' previous ear, but the pig ear was an improvement of the missing ear and permanent scars which were on the side of Marcus' face previously.

Jason sold the larger house and moved closer to the university, three apartments down from where Marcus lived. Despite being the beginning of summer, there was a chill in the air. The two men sat outside on Marcus' patio and ate steak and drank beer. They never spoke about the events at Walnford Plantation, the tunnels of shit, the killer motorcycle gang, the cannibal creatures, or about Jason's wife, Tammy.

The two men handled the stress of the incident in different ways. Marcus internalized the events and suffered tremendous guilt over Brooke Mueller's death. He began working out with a personal trainer and watching his food intake as he lost weight. Marcus also found a girlfriend during those months, and she loved Marcus even if he had a pig ear or not. But Marcus never could sleep through the nights anymore, often waking up in cold sweats seeing the monsters carrying Brooke Mueller away, a woman he only knew for about twelve hours. Medications Marcus found could not take the monsters in his head away, no matter how hard he tried.

While Marcus lost himself in working out and in his love life, Jason handled matters differently. He was in the process of writing a book. He was working on the title but had so far settled on

"The Dubious History and Conspiracies of Walnford Plantation." It was the last few chapters of the book, Jason had the most trouble writing. How much truth should he tell? He thought to himself.

Jason did not date during that time after leaving Walnford Plantation and the jurisdiction surrounding Tunica. No one ever asked him about Tammy Matthews. Tammy's death was almost inconsequential, or worse, it was as if she never existed. It was hard to believe a person could disappear off the face of the earth, and no one would ask about them. Tammy had no living relatives besides her husband, she didn't have a job, and the few friends Tammy did have, she never called, or worse, stole from. Maybe things were better this way, Jason thought to himself in the mornings driving to work or drinking his coffee. Who would believe she was eaten by cannibal creatures anyway?

Sitting on the porch one late fall evening, Jason and Marcus rehashed events from their adventure at Walnford Plantation. This would be the only time they would ever speak about what transpired at Walnford Plantation. Jason sat opposite Marcus in a white lounge chair as music played from inside the house through the screen windows in the kitchen.

"I'm going to ask Jessica to marry me." Marcus said, speaking about his girlfriend.

"Congratulations, buddy. I'm really happy for the both of you." Jason said, taking his beer and clinking his bottle together with Marcus' beer in celebration.

"I know, I haven't known Jessica that long, but she makes me so happy. I don't think I have ever been this happy with someone." Marcus said.

"Good for you." Jason said, taking a sip of his beer smiling.

"When we were in the hospital, you asked me how I was doing Jason. Now it's is my turn to ask you, how are you holding up?" Marcus asked Jason.

"I think about that day at Walnford Plantation all the time. Sometimes I cry, sometimes I'm happy, and most times I wake up knowing that God put a test in my way, and I was able to overcome, to fight, to survive. I did things that day I'm not proud of, but I did these things to survive." Jason said.

"You're alone all the time. That's not healthy. I could ask Jessica if she knows anyone who is single. You could try dating again." Marcus said.

"I never told you this, I never told anyone this, but when I was in the cave and was knocked out, knocked unconscious. Tammy spoke to me. I knew then, lying there on the ground, hearing her voice in my head, she was dead. Tammy spoke to me, motivated me, and told me to get up. It was Tammy's voice I heard. She picked me up, got me moving. If I hadn't heard Tammy's voice, I would be dead now." Jason said.

"It was her fault we were almost killed down there. She hired them to kill us." Marcus said.

"I try and put things into perspective. We were going down there anyway. Those creatures were down there already. Tammy bringing those killers after us in some way may have saved our lives. In some weird symbiotic sort of way. That's what I believe anyway." Jason said.

"I think you've had one too many beers. I'm cutting you off." Marcus said, laughing.

"Seriously, changing subjects, I'm not ready to date. I don't know that I will ever be able to date again. Not after Tammy. But if I ever am, I will let you know." Jason said to his friend.

"Ok, bud. But I am still cutting you off from any more alcohol." Marcus said, still laughing with his friend.

The two men smiled at each other, lifelong friends.

36 - Kingsford Chemical

One year after the events at Walnford Plantation and Joey "Butts" Bishop was supervising the unloading of the chemicals on the flatbed. They called the fat man "Butts" because he always had a cigar butt hanging from his giant lips. None of the workers would call Joey Bishop "Butts" to his face. In addition to being their supervisor, he was also a large scary man.

On this night, Butts was supervising two trailers and two forklifts and two chase cars with eight employees, not counting the drivers of the semi-trucks. They had to work in the dark now since the Environmental Protection Agency knocked on their door months ago and asked where certain chemicals were located. The honest answer was at the bottom of Walnford Plantation lake, but there was no honest answer for people who had search warrants.

Keeping the warehouse clean and disposing of chemicals correctly in an environmentally friendly way had severe financial implications for the company overhead. It was cheaper to put these chemicals into the bottom of a lake bed for a few hundred years. But no longer having the Sheriff on their payroll was another complication. Kingsford Chemicals Vice President of Operations had resigned and relocated with the company's assistance to Costa Rica with a generous employee severance package before he could be subpoenaed.

The company was worried about what former Sheriff Reilly would say about his relationship with Kingsford Chemical. In the end, former Sheriff Reilly accepted a payout he would never receive. On the day of his sentencing, he hadn't cooperated or admitted his guilt in over fifteen charges ranging from bribery, negligence of a government official, conspiracy, fraud, embezzlement, and a slew of other white-collar crimes. Instead of considering the thirty years

Sheriff Reilly served the community into account, the judge decided to make an example of the Sheriff and sentenced him to thirty in prison. Sheriff Reilly would never be able to spend the money Kingsford Chemical gave him to keep quiet. The former Sheriff of Walnford County would die of old age in prison.

On this night at the Walnford Plantation Lake, Butts was supervising the offloading of another thirty barrels of toxic chemicals from the back of the semi-trucks onto a skiff with a small motor. The chemical barrels were then deposited into the center of the lake. Before the Environmental Protection Agency came knocking on Kingsford Chemicals door, the process of getting rid of toxins occurred during daylight hours. Employees would take a hose from the back of their trucks and drain the toxins into the lake. With the Environmental Protection Agency and police lurking about, all the chemicals from the past few months needing to be disposed of would be shipped in this one large shipment.

Butts oversaw the unloading of the semi-trailers and watched as his crew with hand carts and dollies wheeled the containers of chemicals onto the skiff. The skiff would need to make about seven or eight trips to dump all the chemical barrels into the center of the lakebed. The barrels of chemicals were supposed to be non-corrosive, leak-proof, and would allegedly not disintegrate for hundreds of years. Butts thought differently, seeing several barrels that were already rusting away at the bottoms near the edges. This didn't matter to Butts. He would die from old age before any of these containers disintegrated, Butts thought.

Tossing another cigar butt into the lake, Butts pulled another cigar out of his shirt pocket and, producing a lighter, lit another cigar and puffed. When the last chemicals were unloaded into the lake, Butts turned and whistled while waving his right hand in a circle with his index finger pointed to the sky. This was the signal to wrap everything up for the night.

"Let's go. Breakfast is on me." Butts said to the men working underneath him as he started a headcount of his employees. The semi-trucks driving the forklifts back to Kingsford Chemical were already moving away on the dirt road. The headcount was short one person. Was someone missing?

"Has anyone seen Michael? Michael?" Butts asked the men sitting in the two cars waiting to go to breakfast. The men shook their heads, indicating they hadn't seen him.

"He probably hitched a ride back to the factory in one of the trailers." One of the men in the back seat said. The other four men in the car started to agree with one another. He grabbed a ride back. Let's eat. I'm starving, the men in the vehicle repeated in chorus.

Butts looked around in the dark. There was nothing but the lake and the dirt-covered hills. No trees, no tall grass, just dirt and dead reeds. A desolate-looking place.

"Yeah, ok, he probably grabbed a ride back in a trailer." Butts said, getting into the car's front seat and tapping the top of the car with his fingers through the open window.

"Let's go." Butts said.

37- Epilogue

An excerpt from the book
"A History of Walnford Plantation"
by Jason Matthews

Jamison Walnford and his wife Emily boarded the ship Constellation bound for America in Seventeen Ninety-Eight, traveling in the economy class section of the freighter. They had departed from Denmark, but the reason for their departure will forever remain a mystery. Whether the Walnford family was looking for a better life or to escape religious persecution will never be known. The couple arrived in America six weeks later, docking at the maritime Harbor of Virginia.

The couple did not spend much if any time in Virginia other than to buy the necessary horses, food, tools, and travel gear before starting west towards Mississippi, which was then under the territory of Georgia. Georgia at the time claimed the territory west through the Mississippi River. Although Mississippi was not indoctrinated into statehood at that time, the status of the new territory did not deter settlers from expanding as much as the Native Americans, snakes and, disease would allow. Nevertheless, the passage west began not just for the Walnford's but thousands.

Land settlement records indicate Jamison Walnford purchased the tract of land in Georgia during the Yazoo Land Scandal. He would buy the parcel of land just east of Tunica, Mississippi, for fifteen dollars, which was more than a year's salary at that time. How Jamison Walnford came about the funds to purchase travel to America, horses, and land has been lost to time, but we know he was not a rich man. It is most likely he expended his very last penny into making this new settlement with his wife.

The land purchase was fortuitous, as settlers would begin setting up colonies west of the Mississippi following the Louisiana purchase in eighteen hundred and three. These new customers would assist with the selling and purchasing of crops, mainly cotton.

Not much is known about Emily Walnford. She was blond and most likely had just become pregnant at the start of their voyage to America. The travel to where the land Jamison Walnford was rough going; there were cut-away trails from previous expeditions, settlers, and surveyors through the Mississippi areas. Still, Route seventy-two, which is now the main road closest to the Walnford Plantation, did not exist. Located seven to eight miles from the now derelict Walnford plantation, route seventy-two was used by traders from Georgia to take their tobacco products to Mexico.

The land, which would become known as Walnford Plantation, was a natural cul de sac; to this day, it remains surrounded by lofty mountains and a dense forest. A large lake fed by the nearby mountain streams and underground channels would provide water irrigation to the fields and the Walnford family. Because of its location, there is and always has been one road in and one road out.

With the Walnford family arriving at the newly purchased plot of land, the hard work would begin. The land was rich with opportunities, and hard work was the prescription for every day, including the sabbath. Working alone in the fields, Jamison laid out the grid, seeded and planted the crops, mainly food with a section suitable for cotton growing which would become the primary cultivation of the plantation as years went on. Jamison maintained the animals by building makeshift pens until more permanent structures could be erected. Emily Walnford would wash the clothes, prepare meals, and tend to the children.

The first house, a tiny hurried one-room structure, was not completed until after the birth of Jacob. As soon as Jacob was born, Emily would become pregnant again with a second son Jamison junior. The building of the main house on Walnford began shortly after completing temporary living quarters. Farm work on the Walnford Plantation was starting to become profitable. Selling the season's first crops for a tidy profit, Jamison purchased slaves to assist him in the day-to-day farming activities while he turned his attention to building the main dwelling on the Walnford plantation.

The Walnford family home was a massive undertaking, given the nearest resources. Timber and brick were several riding days away, and several thousand tons of stone and bricks would eventually be used to construct the main dwelling. The stone used in the building of the Walnford home can be traced to a quarry in Florida some seven hundred miles away. The two-story house had four upstairs bedrooms, a living and dining room, a kitchen, and a sizeable twenty-foot-high cellar. There were two fireplaces, one in the house's main bedroom and another in the main living room. The front entrance of the Walnford home had grand doors supported by an all-stone wall to support the house. The basement using the same stone as the front of the home was hand dug and then spackled and filled in. Jamison Walnford's work on the main house was completed by eighteen hundred and four. Six years after the purchase of the plantation.

However, Emily and the second son Jamison would never live to see the house completed as both died from malaria symptoms in eighteen hundred and two. Jamison, struck with grief, never remarried.

The work done on the main house was nothing short of extravagant for its time and its location. On December sixteenth, eighteen-eleven, an earthquake struck the Mississippi area. Known as the New Madrid earthquakes, the quake's effects could be felt fifty thousand miles away. The main dwelling of the house, built with a strong foundation of stone and brick, went almost undamaged except for a significant split in the stone basement. Measuring just over five and a half feet in length and just under two feet across the crack in the basement would lead to an underground cavern system. For some unexplained reason, the damaged basement wall would never be patched or repaired.

In eighteen-sixteen, at the young age of fifty, Jamison Walnford passed away. According to the presiding doctor, the exact cause of his death was listed as consumption and was a lengthy ordeal. Then nineteen-year-old Jacob Walnford took over the daily running of the Walnford plantation. Jacob had married the year before to a local woman Mary Surratt then sixteen; she was already pregnant at the time of Jamison Walnford's passing.

Mary Surratt was the middle child of three; her father was a reverend in what would eventually become Commerce Landing. Today Commerce Landing is a literal ghost town used only for farming situated four miles west of the casino resort area of Tunica, Mississippi. In Eighteen-fifteen Commerce Landing was the main shipping port for the northernmost part of the eventual state. Homeschooled throughout her life, Mary Surratt was an educated female and spoke at least three different languages, including French and German.

Together, Jacob Walnford and Mary Surratt would produce four children. If little is known about Jamison and Emily Walnford, even less is known about Jacob Walnford. A reserved man, who always rested on the sabbath, tithed and owned up to all business arrangements. All of the children, when they became adults, resided in the large house at Walnford. Even when taking wives or husbands, they remained at the Walnford house. On May eighth, eighteen-thirty-nine, Mary Surratt Walnford passed away from tuberculous. Jacob would die forty days later on June seventh, eighteen-thirty-nine. His children would say he died of a broken heart, but a fall from a horse may have been a more possible explanation.

The oldest son, Jacob Junior, now became the senior. Born in eighteen-seventeen, Jacob Junior would eventually run the farm when his father died. Marrying Lynn Reynolds in eighteen-thirty-two, their union produced three children. The big house at Walnford expanded with people as the other children produced from Mary Surratt and Jacob Walnford. The two males and one female with families, including children, retained residence at the Walnford house. With Jacob Junior now in charge at Walnford Plantation, the three now-adult children from Jacob and Mary Surrat's union would leave Walnford plantation in the late eighteen forties for California to participate in what would eventually be known as the gold rush. Jacob Junior remained at Walnford Plantation with his wife Lynn, two sons Jacob Jr. and Caleb, and daughter Mary.

In most recovered correspondence received between Jacob and his wife Lynn, the children were always the main focus of all letters, with the topic of state's rights and slavery rearing their ugly heads from time to time. Located at the Tunica Mississippi Museum, several letters and papers from the Walnford family are

194

detailed. Still, none having a premonition so foreboding as the letter dated October twenty-first, eighteen fifty-nine from Jacob Walnford to his wife Lynn while at the capital in Jackson, Mississippi.

My Dearest Lynn,

I hope this letter finds you well. I have received your correspondence and must report the selling of this year's produce is going very well and I may be able to return quicker than I expected.

I am glad you have approved of the match for our son Jacob and his potential bride-to-be. I have been smitten with Evelyn since I was introduced to her and believe she will make a man of our boy. Although two years younger than our son, she is much wiser, more experienced, and older in many ways. I am sure your fondness and admiration of her will grow over time. If only Caleb could find such a suitable wife.

There is talk in the capital of succession as John Brown raided Harper's Ferry in Virginia, stoking the already incensed slaves to liberate themselves. I can only hope this does not spill into a full-on war, and I hope to quell any fears and angst you may perceive by being home sooner than expected. How has the hiring of the additional men around the house to assist with the field workers gone?

I will be home as soon as possible

Love,

Jacob Walnford

October 21, 1859

On January 9, 1861, Mississippi became the second state in the south to secede from the Union. Later that year, at the age of forty-five, Jacob Walnford Sr. would fight for the confederates in the civil war alongside his sons and Jacob and Caleb. Like many Union and Confederate soldiers, they were listed as missing, presumably killed in action, and would never return to the house Jamison Walnford had built sixty years prior.

Thank you for Reading Pyramid of the Prey for Dawn!

Please leave a review on Amazon or Good Reads and let me know what you thought!

Reviews on Amazon or Good Reads help indie authors gain a following and may be the deciding factor influencing someone on whether they will support an author's work. Don't forget to post your review on social media.

Be sure to visit my website http://www.christophermichaelblake.com to receive updates to my book signing schedule, pictures from previous events, giveaways, and my on-going blog detailing my experiences as a writer.

24288511R00116